Birdseed
Cookies

Birdseed Cookies

A FRACTURED

MEMOIR

Janis Jaquith

Library of Congress Number: 00-192823
ISBN #:   Softcover   0-7388-4911-1

Author photo by Jill L. Jaquith.
Cover drawing by Cara Llewellyn.
Janis Jaquith welcomes your comments through her Web site: **www.radioessays.com**

This book was printed in the United States of America.
To order additional copies of this book, contact:
Xlibris Corporation
1-888-7-XLIBRIS
www.Xlibris.com
Orders@Xlibris.com

Contents

PART THREE
WHERE THE HOLY PEOPLE GROW

PART FOUR
I'M JUST SAYING

PART FIVE

BIRDSEED AND A HOT DOG

ILLUSTRATED

BY

CARA

LLEWELLYN

ACKNOWLEDGEMENTS

Without the encouragement and cooperation of Jim Davis, local host of Morning Edition at WVTF, not one of these essays would have been written.

And, without the forbearance of my family and friends, there would have been little to write about.

INTRODUCTION

I was gnawing on my thumbnail, late one sticky spring afternoon, when it dawned on me—we had all developed nervous tics.

In the chair next to mine sat a willowy young black woman who had taken to obsessively twirling a lock of hair around her index finger while staring intently at nothing.

A woman on the other side of me, her slack, pasty face a study in the effects of sleep-deprivation, was doing the hair-twirling thing, plus she sat with her legs crossed while ferociously shaking her dangling foot from side to side.

A guy from India, arms folded tightly across his chest, was rocking back and forth.

We had, all of us, endured our first year of graduate school, and the classroom was packed with people twitching, rocking, tapping, nail-chewing—I was inhabiting a scene right out of *One Flew Over the Cuckoo's Nest.*

We didn't start out this way. In September we had arrived, fresh-faced, right out of college. All mentally healthy (near as I could tell) and eager to immerse ourselves in the study of linguistics.

Now, if you've served any time in graduate school, you know that the first order of business when dealing with new recruits is to wring the enthusiasm and curiosity right out of them. Listen carefully—there's a faint whisper that sifts down and settles into everything you do there: *So, you love school, do you? You think it's fun to learn? Just can't get enough? Well, we'll see about that.*

Each professor pretends not to know that you really do have other classes besides his, honest. An academic hazing, that's what it is. How much pressure, how much sleeplessness can you stand, and for how long? And some of us had teaching fellowships, to boot, with classes to prepare for every day.

As I observed my neurotic classmates that spring day, each little fidget was amplified, like a ticking clock in a silent room that grows louder and louder until you cover your ears and run shrieking into the street.

In a blinding stupor, I faced the blackboard, where sounds were captured in the phonetic alphabet with colored chalk. I blinked, and each blink, during the blackness, was a flashback to all the other classrooms I'd been stuck in throughout my life.

Blink: Chalk squeaks as Mrs. Prolman painstakingly inscribes the alphabet on the blackboard.

Blink: Third grade. Long division on the board. Numbers stacked up and sliding off to the left. If those were blocks they'd fall over . . . *Janis, what's the answer?* Ah, jeez.

Blink: Seventh grade, and my eyelids are made of lead as Miss Spencer drones on while diagramming a sentence—a black-and-white map to nowhere.

Blink: Ninth grade, a sweltering summer-school classroom where, for the third time, algebra doesn't make so much as a dent in my mind. I throw up in the waste basket, and they let me go home.

Blink: Freshman biology in a crowded, airless lecture hall where I escape internally, pretending my bicycle and I are coasting down the road from Gloucester to Rockport, salt air inflating my lungs.

For eighteen years–eighteen years!—I have been holed up in a classroom, dreaming of escape. Why am I here?

At that moment, my eyes scarcely focused and staring toward the phonetic squiggles on the blackboard, I made a decision. This path I was on, it was tailor-made to make me crazy.

A little voice that had been waiting patiently in the murkiest depths of my mind seized this opportunity to step forward:

Wise up! Life in the slow lane—think about it.

Well, the University of Pennsylvania must have perceived my epiphany, because they made the transition simple: Mere weeks after my decision, I failed my qualifier exam (twice) and was free to do anything on Earth except pursue an advanced degree in linguistics at Penn.

I knew exactly what I wanted to do. And, let me tell you, this was not a fashionable choice to make in 1977. I was supposed to want a career that would bring me money—my own money. A career that would win me prestige so that I could show the previous generation of women how they had wasted their lives behind an apron.

The thing is, I couldn't wait to hold a baby in my arms. And, staying home and taking care of a baby—how hard could that be? I envisioned huge expanses of free time: time to read, time to sew, time to bake chocolate-chip cookies. My stress-free life stretched out in front of me.

That's when the gods elbowed one another, guffawed and said, "Hey, let's send her twins . . . twin boys."

This was kind of like starting grad school again, only I couldn't weasel out by flunking a test.

As the years passed, I watched my friends earn their advanced degrees and move up the success ladder. Sometimes I envied them their money and freedom, but mostly I was grateful to have a career that allowed me to do cartwheels in public.

As the twins got older and were joined by a sister, I discovered that even stay-at-home motherhood was becoming too much of a fast-lane existence.

Harry and I looked around at the traffic, the crime, and the unbroken wall of aluminum siding that our neighborhood had turned into, and said, "Let's get out of here."

And so, when the twins were on the verge of high school, and Jill was ready for fourth grade, we wrenched them away from their schools and friends and lives in the claustrophobia-inducing planned community of Columbia, Maryland.

We plunked the family down in what our kids called "the middle of nowhere" in the foothills of the Blue Ridge Mountains of Virginia.

You know how good it feels to take off a too-tight pair of shoes at the end of the day? That's what it felt like to move out to the country.

People are happier here. They aren't all jammed together, and the scenery is gorgeous. What's not to be happy about? As a result, people are nicer to one another. If I put my signal on to change lanes, someone in the next lane will slow down a bit to create a gap and let me in. Anyplace else, you wouldn't even use your signal. That's like tipping off the enemy to your battle plan—that's when they close ranks.

Over the past few years, I have had the great good luck to have a whole slew of my essays broadcast on the radio. And, amazingly enough, there are listeners who seem to like my little stories about this allegedly stress-free life of mine.

I hope you like them, too.

PART ONE

JIGGEDY JOG

CONFESSIONS OF A

BABYSITTER

When I was thirteen years old, I babysat for a child who was invisible.

A neighbor had called my mother to see if I'd be interested in taking care of her son, Ralphie. Ralphie was a baby and . . . Well, that's about all I ever knew about Ralphie.

Since he was their first child, it was the kind of household where everyone tiptoes around so's not to wake the baby. I was the youngest in my family, and nobody tiptoed—ever. As the baby myself, I had never even held a baby, so I was scared to death that old Ralphie might wake up. What would I do then?

I walked through their back door into what felt like a church, with a silence that was palpable. The only sounds were grownups whispering and shushing. Baby powder and disinfectant hung in the air like incense.

Ralphie's room—the *sanctum sanctorum*—was darkened. I was taken only as far as the hallway, where the mother gestured in the direction of the infant, but it was clear we were not going to approach him. Ralphie was not to be disturbed.

After Mr. and Mrs. Burpee left, (that was their name, I swear: Burpee) I settled into the living room, paging through their collection of record albums. And, keeping the volume very low, I made my way through their stash of Johnny Mathis records. No way would Johnny Mathis wake up anybody. On the coffee table was, as I remember it, a very racy book. I forget the author, but the name of the book was *Candy*, and Ringo Starr was in the movie version.

Oh, yeah, it's coming back to me now. It was a racy book, all right.

I had a very nice time that night, what with the Johnny Mathis music and the absorbing literature. The Burpees came back before midnight and paid me a dollar an hour, which was good money for the mid-sixties, let me tell you.

Well, I went back to Ralphie's house many times over the next couple of years, and it was interesting to check out the current photographs of the little guy, just to see who I was getting paid to babysit for, because *I never, ever did lay eyes on that child.*

Oh, yeah . . . it was a racy book, all right.

And one time, the Burpees were going out with their neighbors from across the street, who had a newborn baby. Rather than hire two sitters, they brought their baby over to the Burpee's house, hired me, and paid me double.

I never laid eyes on *that* baby, either.

Enough time had passed that I wondered whether this might be a trick, and maybe there *was* no extra baby that night.

But nobody ever said anything about it to me. They just put a thick wad of bills in my hand and said goodnight.

Years passed; I grew up and had my own babies. (Twins, which, come to think of it, may be a kind of penance for having neglected old Ralphie.) I was about twenty-eight years old when I drove past the Burpee's house. The name was still on the mailbox, and there was this lanky young man emerging from an old Volkswagen; he was sort of unfolding himself. Must've been over six feet tall.

I caught a glimpse of his face. It was the face on all those baby and toddler portraits from their living room wall: Ralphie Burpee. At last.

I considered waving, but thought better of it.

After all, we've never met.

WHY I DON'T SKI

I can't hear my own screams, that's how loud the snowmaking machine is. Like a jet engine thirty feet over my head. I fell over, and now, I can't get up.

I was born in New England, so people think I must know how to ski. Well, I don't. I come from a long line of people who don't ski. My parents didn't ski. These were people who struggled through the Great Depression and World War II. Just getting through life was risk enough for them; they didn't need to invent ways to put themselves in danger.

It wasn't until I was eighteen, and passing through ski country during the winter, that I discovered whole families of skiers staying at expensive inns. These were families with three and four kids, and everybody was outfitted in the kind of ski clothing that can only be called "togs."

I had discovered a parallel universe of people who looked like me, but who lived a whole different kind of life.

These were the kind of people who use "summer" as a verb. As in, "we summer in Bar Harbor."

I summered down the street in Leslie Dluzneiski's cellar or else I summered out back, in the swamp, catching tadpoles.

I wintered in pretty much the same places.

The swamp behind my house wasn't such a bad place to spend the winter. It froze solid, and was a great place to skate on with my double-runners. A good, long stretch of unbroken ice in the swamp would be about four or five feet. It was step, step, glide . . . Grab a tree; step, step, glide . . . Clutch a bunch of cattails.

It wasn't until I slipped below the Mason-Dixon Line that I finally dared to ski. I took the beginner's lesson and it was okay. In fact, it was thrilling. I was gliding along in slow motion on the slightest of inclines, but for me, that was breathtaking. As I inched along, I had visions of us all—my husband, me, and our three kids—becoming habitués of the slopes at Wintergreen. Staying at the inn. Wearing togs.

I could be one of those people. I could get used to using "summer" as a verb.

Just minutes later, I'm happily sailing along when suddenly, pure whiteness and a deafening roar envelop me. I'm falling, but there's no up or down, all is whiteness. I'm falling through space. Isn't this what death is like? Except, I'm screaming, and aren't you supposed to feel peaceful when the white light shows up?

I hit the ground and my skis splay outward, holding my legs in unnatural positions. I'm stuck. I holler for help, but who could hear me? Even *I* can't hear me over the roar of the snowmaking machine mere yards over my head.

As the *faux* snow accumulates on me I imagine myself buried in the stuff. People, unknowing, will ski over me all winter until springtime, when—perfectly preserved in my togs—my body will be discovered, like that glacier guy they found in the Alps a few years ago.

Then, miraculously, my daughter appears and rescues her mother—her screaming, crying, hysterical mother.

Look, let's just forget the whole thing. I was not cut out
for stuff like this. You have to be to the manner born. I was to
the swamp born.

And you won't catch me using "summer" as a verb, I'll
tell you that.

INTELLIGENT LIFE

It was after midnight. I lay in the bottom bunk, my arm reaching out to the old radio on my nightstand. It was a brown plastic box warmed from within by glowing vacuum tubes, and the speaker was covered with disintegrating cloth. I lowered the volume a little before twisting the knob to find a new station. I didn't want the static and that wide warble that comes between stations to wake up Patty in the top bunk. She'd yell at me to turn it off, or worse, she'd tell Mum.

This was the best part of my day. I lay there in the dark with just the glowing radio dial and the stars out my window to look at.

Every night, on WBZ, I listened to the *Bob Kennedy Contact* show and he had on people like Edgar Rowe Snow telling us ghost stories about places right there in Massachusetts. Or Jeanne Dixon predicting the future. Later, I'd twist my way through the radio spectrum, discovering in the static and warble a station all the way from Indiana, and one from Montreal, where the announcer was speaking French. I discovered news, music, stories.

I was by myself, but I wasn't alone.

The rest of my day was school and homework and some stupid TV programs. What a relief it was to reach for that smooth knob—it felt like I was scanning the universe for signs of intelligent life. I couldn't find it in my *house*, that's for sure. My parents were so boring. And not in my school. My teachers were pathetic. The same stuff every day. Get out your homework. Open your book . . . Boring, boring.

But at night, in the dark, my thoughts spooled out into the universe like fishing line following a hook and lure. And which was more exciting: discovering something new, or the *anticipation* of discovering something new? Hard to say.

Well, decades have passed, and now I spend hours every day reaching out to my computer, the transparent blue plastic cover warmed by something mysterious within. I use it to write stories, to scan the world for news, and believe it or not, I'm also searching for intelligent life in the universe. Really.

There's an organization of radio astronomers who're scanning the universe, looking for radio signals from alien civilizations. Just like Jody Foster in *Contact*.

Only now, instead of just using the astronomers' computers to analyze all that information gathered from the heavens, someone had the brilliant idea of using the collective power of millions of our personal computers. And my trusty iMac is analyzing the radio signals that are coming from my own teeny-tiny sliver of sky. Together, we make up the mother of all computers. The project is called SETI, the Search for Extra-Terrestrial Intelligence.

If I don't touch my keyboard for a while, my SETI screen saver comes on, and it's during that idle time that the SETI software is doing its thing, crunching those numbers—and if ET does indeed phone home, the computers just might intercept it.

And, from time to time, the SETI program *does* phone home, downloading and uploading, hooking in with all the other computers.

This stuff is a long way from listening in the dark, searching for intelligent life in Indiana.

I like to think that this generation of radio astronomers were also kids who were awake when everyone else was asleep, twisting through the radio spectrum, wondering what else was out there.

ATTENTION DEFICIT DISORDER—WHO KNEW?

I'm lying on my back in the sunshine, holding my little pink elephant up against the clouds—pretending we're flying—when a shadow falls over me. It's my grandfather. He brings his face closer, right into my playpen, and he's smiling and saying something to me, something sing-songy. I turn away from him, hoping he'll just go away. This playpen is mine. When I'm in here, nobody bothers me. I get to think and do anything I please. My grandfather goes away and now I can get back to flying with my elephant.

***

I hear my father's voice. He's home from work. I run to my hiding place, a new one. I try not to giggle and give myself away as my father looks for me, saying, "Where's my little girl? Where's my Janny?" This is my best hiding place yet. I'm in the bathroom, buried under laundry in the clothes hamper. My hiding place is too good, and after a while Daddy gives up.

I decide that I sort of like it in the laundry hamper. It smells funny, but I like the way it muffles the sound. My father's voice sounded far away, and now I should be able to hear my parents talking as they sit down at the kitchen table for their daily cocktail. But I hear nothing. And I like it.

***

I'm sitting at a desk in first grade. The teacher's standing up in front of us, and she's talking and talking about something or other. Her glasses are hanging from a chain around her neck. Like a necklace, but not really. She's wearing one of those big fake roses—it's pinned to her dress. I think my grandmother has one of those.

I look down at my desk: There are all these little squares of green paper. I don't know where they came from. Each square has a number on it. What am I supposed to do with those? I look around at the other kids and a hot stab of panic shoots through my chest. All the other kids are doing something special with those numbers. They all know what to do. Now the teacher is moving up and down the aisles, licking little gold stars and pressing them to the foreheads of the kids who know what they're doing. She goes right past me.

I don't belong here. I don't know how I got here. I don't know what I'm supposed to do. I'd go home . . . but I don't know how to do that, either.

***

First grade is better now. I know where everything is. When I get here in the morning, I know where to hang up my coat, I know where Mrs. Prolman keeps the paper, and where to find a box of those terrific fat red pencils. I feel like I belong here. Best of all, I know right where my desk is.

Reading group is wonderful. I'm very good at it, it turns out. When it's my turn to read, everyone's quiet and I can read aloud perfectly, faster than anyone else.

But now, reading group is over and we're back at our seats. Now I have to take out my *Think and Do Book*. That's the workbook that goes with those Dick, Jane, and Sally stories. I try to tell people how much I hate this stupid *Think and Do* workbook, but nobody listens to me—nobody cares about how much I hate to do this workbook.

I know the story, okay? I read it. I got it. So why do I have to answer questions about it in this stupid workbook? I try to write the answers, but my letters come out all wrong and so I erase and it leaves a messy smudge, so I erase harder and make a hole in the page. It's like this for every answer, just about, and on every page. Sometimes I tell Mrs. Prolman I can't find my workbook, or I hide it over on the bookshelves. But she always finds it. I stare at the page with its gray smudges and holes and I imagine lighting a match and burning it up right there on my desk.

Trying to do what I'm supposed to do in this workbook is like when my father sits down at the kitchen table to figure out his taxes, that's what it's like. Or when my mother sits in that same chair, doing stuff with her checkbook and bills and then she stops and buries her face in both her hands. It's like that. Only every day.

***

I'm in third grade, and do I ever love the setup in this classroom. It's a real old school and the desks and chairs are screwed into the floor. The rows stay straight all the time. I love this. And in the back of the classroom is a bookshelf with a collection of books that are, like, fifth- or sixth-grade reading level. If I get my work done, I can go back there and read anything I want, and I don't have to answer any stupid questions about it. Pure joy.

I just got off the bus, came in and hung up my raincoat. I settle into my seat and look up at the side blackboard. Oh, no. There's before school work on the board. This is as unfair as anything I can think of. *Before* school work? Give me a break. Let me catch my breath, for heaven's sake. I take a good look at it and feel the bottom drop out of my stomach: It's a word problem, with pints and quarts and gallons. Oh, my God. I don't know which way is up. I take out a piece of paper and at least write my name on it. Mrs. Donahue is going to call me a featherhead again, I just know it. I don't know where to start—I don't know how to think about this problem. And she has explained this stuff to us over and over.

What if I'm retarded? I hope they don't put me in special class. I will die if they put me in special class.

For the zillionth time, Mrs. Donahue is at the front of the class, explaining about pints and quarts and gallons. She's doing the problem that was on the side board this morning. I am trying so hard to pay attention, it practically hurts. But trying to pay attention feels like I'm trying to hold a beachball under water. The effort is too great, and it feels so unnatural.

I'm sorry, everybody, but I just can't do it.

I allow the beachball to pop up into its own realm, where it belongs. What a relief!

Mrs. Donahue's voice sounds far away now, a kind of honking music with its own rising and falling rhythm. When she moves her mouth, there are all these little wrinkles that radiate out from her lips, especially the top one.

All this talk about pints and gallons makes me think about chocolate milk. The way it's so thick and tastes so good. I wonder what it would taste like if I put chocolate milk on my Sugar Crisp in the morning.

From somewhere far away, I hear my name. Ah, jeez. How

did she know I wasn't listening? I was looking right at her. So, what's the answer, she wants to know? Everyone's looking at me and smirking, including Mrs. Donahue. The answer must be ridiculously obvious to any normal person. The boy behind me whispers "retard" and I *will* myself to die.

***

It's morning. I'm sitting on the floor of my room, feeling a little chilly in just my underwear. I'm stacking up my glossy encyclopedias, fanning them outward until they look like a sweeping, fancy staircase, the kind Cinderella ran down. I think it looks really good.

My mother comes to the door. She looks like she's crazy. Her face is all twisted and mad. She sounds like she's strangling when she says, "The bus comes in five minutes. You have been in here for half an hour. What have you been doing?" Hm. Half an hour? That sounds improbable to me. It feels like about three minutes.

***

I'm standing at the bottom of Vonnie Erickson's back porch. Vonnie's a year older than me, and I really want her to be my friend. I'm not sure how to go about this be-my-friend thing, so I figure persistence is my best bet. She's at her kitchen window, saying, "No! I don't want to come out and play with you!"

"Are you sure?" I say, for perhaps the twentieth time. Vonnie's face disappears from the window. Somehow, I can't seem to shut up. "Honest and truly?" I say.

From somewhere in the kitchen I hear her say, "Yes!"

"Bably and booley?" I cleverly reply.

Her face appears again, just long enough to shut the window. Oh, well. I had a pretty good idea that I was being obnoxious, but I didn't know how else to be. I couldn't stop myself. I would have used another script, if I'd had one. Persistence usually pays off with my parents and brother and sister. They'll do most anything to get me to shut the hell up, as my big brother says. He's in college.

***

I'm in fourth grade and the difference between my smart side and my dumb side is getting bigger all the time. I'm one of the best readers and we've been writing these stories lately and we're allowed to just make things up and write about them. Just make things up! This is great.

What's not so great is that I get marked down because my handwriting is so bad. It's not like Mr. Sweeney can't read it, because he can, and he really likes my stories, but he puts me down a whole grade because he says it looks like I wrote it with my foot instead of my hand.

I try, I really do, but my pencil just will not do what I tell it to. It's like everyone else is some kind of super-duper artist, capturing these letters and words on paper, and I can't even draw a straight line. All anyone says about my handwriting is: If you'd just be more careful. If you'd just slow down. If you'd just try. Like, if I was a better person, I'd have better penmanship.

I look at other kids' handwriting and I think: How do they *do* it?

***

Just the sight of math paper makes me sick to my stomach. It's small and beige and flecked with tiny woody bits. If you don't think about what it's for, you might actually like math paper. There are no lines so it would be great for drawing on, or folding into something neat. By the time I'm finished with it, though, you wouldn't even want to look at it.

We're supposed to be real whizzes at long division by fourth grade, but I can't even line up the numbers on top of each other to make a column, and I end up adding the wrong stuff together. Being stuck in the middle of one of those problems is like being lost in a department store when you're little. There's no way you're getting out of it by yourself. It's hopeless.

***

For years, or since first grade, anyway, I have enjoyed many happy hours sitting in boxes. You know, those big ones that TVs or whatever come in. Give me a box, a light, and a book and I'll be happy for hours. Now, does that sound weird to you? I don't think so.

When we get a good box, I go down cellar where we keep the Christmas decorations, and I get the cord and bulb that go into our light-up snowman. You can just twist it right out and use that light any way you want to.

I make a hole in the top of the box and drop that light bulb down into it. I use one of those aluminum-foil, chicken-pot-pie plates for a shade. Just poke a hole in that, too. I crawl in the box through the flaps, which I have on one end, and I just pull the flaps up, and there I am! This is the best place to be. You can read, or draw, or just think straight—which is great.

Well, my mother thinks I'm nuts. She worries about me sitting in the box all the time. A few weeks ago, she took me to the doctor's office, she was so worried. It wasn't even time for a checkup or shots or anything.

So, Dr. MacDougall puts me on the scale and takes my blood pressure, looks in my ears and all that jazz. My mother's watching the whole thing, like Dr. MacDougall is gonna find something in my ear that will explain why I like to sit in the box. When he's done, my mother says, "Well?" And Dr. MacDougall shrugs his shoulders and says, "If she wants to sit in the box, let her sit in the box."

Anyway, the box mysteriously disappeared a few days later, so I had to move into the closet. My sister (she's in high school) is ready to kill me. She says it's her closet too and I ruin all her clothes by squishing them all to one side of the closet.

Like I care. I have a clubhouse in that closet.

The walls are this wonderful, smooth white plaster. It's great for writing on. I wrote up on the wall all the different jobs in the club—you know, president, treasurer, secretary, members . . . And then I filled in my name under each one. I get along very well with everyone in the club.

***

My fifth-grade classroom is a nightmare. The desks are all over the place. Nothing is nailed to the floor, and I never know what the place is gonna look like from one day to the next. I hate this. It makes me feel like I'm mentally ill, or something. I just get so confused—it's hard to think about anything else. Mr. Fratianni—he's my teacher—he likes to change the place around all the time, and it drives me crazy, I mean it. How would he like it if his wife rearranged the kitchen all the time? It would be hard to get anything done in there, wouldn't it? He'd never know where anything was.

Today, Mr. Fratianni had us in groups of four—four desks all pushed together and facing each other. Actually I kind of like this most of the time, because there's always someone to talk to or poke or make goofy drawings for when things get boring, which is most of the time. I don't get much done, but I'm having a good time.

***

As it happens, I'm in the principal's office right now. I have to stand with my back right next to, but not touching, the side of the file cabinet. I have to stay here until recess is over. This is humiliating.

Here's what happened: I was at my lunch table in the cafeteria, sitting next to Claire Fogg. Claire finishes her hard-boiled egg—which stunk, by the way—and she takes out a Hershey bar for dessert. It just so happens that I am crazy about Hershey bars. I watch her slide that long silver rectangle out from the brown paper sleeve and then she opens it up, and I can smell it.

It's the kind of Hershey bar that has the little lines pressed into it, so you can, like, share it easily. Claire breaks off about a third of it when she looks up at me watching her. She gets this squinty look in her eyes and just shakes her head, as if to say: Forget it—I'm not sharing this with anyone.

The next thing I know, the rest of that Hershey bar is in my mouth, all of it. And it tastes so good, you wouldn't believe it.

And then, Claire is yelling and fake-crying and it turns out that there was a teacher who saw the whole thing. All the teacher kept saying was, "What were you thinking? Why did you do that?"

I couldn't explain it to her, but the truth is, there was no "thinking" part. I went right from wanting that candy bar, to chewing it. Boom. I don't know what happened to the part where I was supposed to consider whether to do it or not.

This happens to me all the time. I call out answers and questions in class when it's not time to. I interrupt like crazy, even when I don't want to. Other people don't do this, and it makes me wonder how they know when it's the right time to speak up, because I know that if I don't say what's on my mind right away, I'll forget it. And sometimes the ideas are jumping into my mind so fast, it's like popcorn popping. And I don't know which idea to say out loud first. They all seem important. So, I'll end up blurting out something that isn't really what I wanted to say at all.

Which drives me crazy. And while I'm on the subject of memory, I don't know how other kids always seem to bring the right books home for homework, and then they actually get it all done, *and* they can find it the next day. This amazes me. It's like the handwriting thing, I guess. Just another talent I don't have.

***

I'm pretty sure now that I'm not retarded, but I wonder if I'm going senile. I'm serious. Is that possible in fifth grade? I read about lots of weird diseases every month in Reader's Digest, and I wonder if I have some of those diseases, like being senile. I'm always forgetting things and nobody believes me. They say I do it for attention. Yeah, right. Like I need more attention. I'll forget my homework, I'll forget where I took off one of my shoes, I'll forget to come home . . .

And to show you how messed up I really am, I'll remember something one day, forget it the next, and then remember it the third day! Like, if you asked me right now what nine times eight is, I really couldn't tell you. But I knew it yesterday, and chances are it'll come back to me tomorrow. If that's not senile, I don't know what is.

Anyway, one good thing about standing here all alone in the principal's office is I have all this free time to think straight.

Not such a bad deal, for a weirdo like me.

JESUS WOULD LET THE AIR OUT OF HIS TIRES

Have you seen those cloth bracelets with the letters WWJD woven into them? It stands for What Would Jesus Do?

When I was a kid, the nuns used to say that to us in Sunday school. It was supposed to guide us into the highest moral choice.

However, whenever I see one of those bracelets, I don't usually think about high moral choices. I think about my mother.

One day, when I was in high school, my mother was fuming over a problem we were having with our neighbor. The divorced woman across the street from us was frequently entertaining a new beau. Her paramour drove a truck, an enormous semi that was easily bigger than our little ranch house. When he was in town, he would arrive at night and park his rig on the street, right across from our house, just yards away from my mother's bedroom window.

In the mornings, in anticipation of his departure, he

would turn on the engine and allow the truck to warm up over the course of half an hour before taking his leave. Maybe that's how long their romantic goodbye took, I really don't know. But the fumes from his diesel engine spewed from the truck and enveloped our entire house, seeping in past locked windows and bolted doors.

We were sitting in the living room one night, my mother, my boyfriend, and I, watching Johnny Carson, when we heard the familiar rumble, and that enormous steel rectangle slid across our picture window, filling it.

The driver turned his engine off right away—he wasn't going anywhere until dawn. Nevertheless, the blood rose into Mum's face like mercury in a thermometer. No need to ask what was wrong. She was thinking about this ten-ton alarm clock lurking outside her bedroom. About that arrogant, vertical exhaust pipe that stood ready to inject its diesel venom into our home.

Both Mum and I were thinking that if Dad were still alive, he'd march right over there and let that son-of-a-bitch know what he could do with that truck of his. My boyfriend was no substitute for Dad, that's for sure. He found it amusing that Mum was so upset. As Mum glared out the window, my boyfriend smirked and said, "Well now, Mrs. Jaquith, what would Jesus do?"

Still looking out the window, and without missing a beat, Mum said, "Jesus'd let the air out of his tires."

We laughed, but she turned to us, and in all seriousness explained that letting some—not all—of the air out of his tires wouldn't hurt the tires, wouldn't hurt the driver or anyone else. But he would get the message that surely there are better places to park a semi for the night.

No more was said about this, but after I said goodnight to my boyfriend at the back door, it was many minutes before I heard his car engine start up.

The next morning, our house vibrated as usual, and we

awoke to the familiar smell of exhaust fumes. Before I had a chance to look out the window and see what shape those tires were in, the truck was gone.

And, it never came back.

As the years have passed, I've often thought about what happened that night. I hope the truck wasn't damaged, and I hope nobody got hurt. At the time, it seemed ludicrous to imagine that Jesus would have handled the same situation with anything but patience and understanding.

But recently, I've been thinking about that unpleasantness in the temple with the moneychangers. Jesus overthrew their tables and poured out the changers' money, saying, "Make not my father's house a house of merchandise."

So now, whenever I come across that phrase, "What would Jesus do?" I think, "Jesus'd let the air out of his tires."

THE LAST TIME I SAW PARIS

My house is littered with half-finished projects that seemed like a good idea at the time. Like the box of oil paints. I took a few classes, painted one painting, and that was it.

Whenever I come across that box of paints, I tell myself: Someday.

I even dropped out of college after one week. One week. It took an entire winter of working for Fanny Farmer in a cinderblock warehouse to convince me to go back the following September.

I went back, and I'm glad I did, because I was given a wonderful opportunity—to spend my junior year in Paris. Back home, my world had been pretty narrow. In Paris, my world—my life—was expansive and fascinating.

I went to the opera, to the ballet. I walked past Notre Dame every afternoon. Occasionally, I'd drop in on the huge, curving display of Monet's water lilies. I walked along the street eating fabulous pastries.

At the end of the year, when it was time to go home, I thought: Why would I want to go home? I'd even had a job offer in Paris. Something clerical in a public relations firm. But it was a job. In Paris. Who could pass that up?

I got along so well in Paris that Parisians were *nice* to me. I swear.

There came the day, in early August, when it was time to either confirm my reservation on the SS France for the mid-August sailing to New York, or cash in my ticket.

I can still remember the long walk from the subway to the French Lines office. To get there, I had to pass the Paris Opéra. I had been to the opera house many times with my friends Florence and Maura, who were also American students.

I looked up at that ornate building and thought about the time I fainted during a performance of *Swan Lake* and had to leave before it was over. I was way up in the cheap seats, standing at the back, because these particular seats had no view of the stage, believe it or not. And it was hot up there.

As I came to, I heard Florence's voice. She was asking if anyone had a program, so she could fan my face with it. I opened my eyes to see all these concerned French people fanning me with Kleenexes and hankies. Of course no one had a program. People who pay a buck for their tickets are not going to pay five bucks for one of those glossy opera programs.

As I walked past the opera house, I kept my hand in my pocket, touching the little folder that held my ticket.

I got closer to the shipping office, and I was thinking: I'll do it. I'll stay. I belong here.

As I pushed open the heavy glass door I thought about all the things I'd begun in my life but never finished. Assignments, projects, relationships.

When the woman behind the counter said, "Would you like to sail on August sixteenth?" what came out of my mouth was, "Yes."

I went back to Boston and earned my bachelor's degree, telling myself that I can always decide to go back and live in Paris. After all, it's a long life.

That was twenty-three years ago.

This past Christmas, Maura sent me a coffee-table book, a picture book of Paris. Now, I flip through the photographs of the Latin Quarter and Notre Dame and I tell myself: Someday.

BREAKTHROUGH

Last Sunday, I read an article in the newspaper. In this article, famous people—make that *smart*, famous people—each wrote a few paragraphs about books that changed their lives. Some of them wrote about books that changed their lives during their early years.

Now, these are the kind of people who were reading Jane Austen when I was reading Nancy Drew. The books mentioned were by Updike and Merton and Nabokov. I just learned how to pronounce Na-BO-kov a few months ago. The whole time I was reading *Lolita*, I assumed the author was NAB-uh-kov. Who knew?

The book that changed my life was the first book I ever read. In my first-grade classroom, we read *Dick, Jane, and Sally,* but those were mostly pictures with a few asinine exclamations below.

At home, I had a slim copy of *The Elves and the Shoemaker.* It had been a birthday gift, one that was overlooked until now. When I first resolved to read it, I flipped through, and on the fourth page a hot twinge of dread shot through my stomach as I found an unbroken expanse of text and realized I would have to decipher that whole page without benefit of *any* illustrations.

After I had a few more weeks of reading instruction under my belt, I brought the book to my mother one evening and attempted to read it aloud to her, as she had read books to me.

Kneeling next to her, I place the book on my mother's knee. I read the first three pages confidently, since there are no more than two or three sentences on each page. Then, I turn to the dreaded page four. I take a deep breath and force myself along that rocky trail of text.

About a third of the way through, an amazing thing happens. Instead of deciphering the text, it feels as though the text is revealing itself to me. Those impenetrable shapes are arranging themselves into real words, beckoning to me, inviting me to follow them.

I make it through that page and the next page and the next and the next, astonished that there is a *story* there, a story that had been there all along, waiting for me to recognize it—as though I had always known how to do it, but had somehow forgotten.

Until that moment, the printed page had been a flat, opaque surface. Now, it had become transparent, a surface to be broken and plunged into, a hidden landscape to explore and become lost in.

How could anyone's life be the same after *that?*

JIGGEDY JOG

I'm driving down the street very slowly. My kids are in the back seat, begging me to hurry up and get away from here. I stop in front of the house. I don't know who lives here, but I can't take my eyes off the place.

This house—this little ranch-style tract house with the carport and the picture window—is the house I lived in from the time I was five years old until I got married. Before this we lived in Vermont, and other places, but this was our first real house.

I notice that the window by the back door, under the carport, still has a big air conditioner hanging out of it.

I have vivid memories of kissing my boyfriend goodnight—for a very long time—below that window, the air conditioner humming above us.

A man comes out on the front porch. I put the car into drive and prepare to take off, but he smiles and waves as he walks toward us. I tell him that this is where I grew up.

His name is Gino. He escorts us into my house and introduces his wife, Robin. Such good-hearted, welcoming people.

So, why am I annoyed with them for changing my house?

Here in the kitchen, they've covered the blonde pine cabinets with white paint. They've replaced the countertops, and the pink-and-black-striped linoleum has given way to beige No-Wax flooring.

I feel uneasy, like this is a strange dream. In third grade, I dreamed that I came home from school, and as I approached the front porch, I noticed that there were different flowers and bushes out front. Long-established bushes. When I walked into the house, I found a strange family living there. And they'd always lived there. Not only did I not belong there, I didn't belong anywhere.

And that's what it feels like as I walk through this house. I don't belong in my house.

I tell myself: Get a grip. What did you expect? To find Mum standing at the stove, melting butter and chocolate to make brownies? To find Patty sitting at the table in the dinette, doing her homework?

Gino leads us down cellar to his workbench. Fan belts and tire chains hang from the wooden beam overhead. My boys are especially impressed by this room. They're ten years old and are happy in a room that's messy and filled with dangerous objects.

Gino grins and points upward. I don't know what he's pointing at.

And then I see it. Nailed to the beam is a green license plate. Vermont, 1954.

My father nailed that up there when we first moved in. Unbelievable. It's still there.

And then, ceremoniously, as though he's been waiting for this moment, Gino reaches up and pulls down the license plate. The nail holding it drops to the cement floor. Gino hands the license plate to me, saying, "You should have this. It belongs to you."

Now Jackson's on his hands and knees, retrieving the nail. He looks at it, then holds it close to his heart. To Gino, he says, "My grandfather was the last person to touch this nail." This is a grandfather that Jackson never knew.

During the ten-hour drive from Massachusetts back to Maryland, the memory of this house-tour starts to fade as I imagine myself, tomorrow, in my big colonial house, melting butter and chocolate for brownies while my kids do their homework at the kitchen table.

And I know exactly where I'm going to put that license plate.

SILENT REBELLION

The year is 1960. I'm eight years old, sitting on a hard pew between my parents. It's a hot, sticky summer Sunday. Wide-open windows on either side of the church let in a warm breeze that carries the thick scent of freedom.

I'm leaning against my father's broad arm, willing the breeze to blow harder and cool my face, when the congregation rises in unison—a field of faithful starlings responding to an unseen signal. I take my place among them, and perched on top of the padded kneeler, I come up almost as high as my parents' shoulders.

I am enveloped by grownups—a solid wall of dark suits and flowered dresses all around me. There's comfort in this, even on a stifling hot day. The priest speaks the first two words, "Our Father . . . " and they all join him. " . . . Who art in heaven, hallowed be Thy name . . . "

The low rumble of grownup voices surrounds me. I join them. "Thy kingdom come, Thy will be done . . . " The joining of my voice with theirs sets up a harmonic vibration that resounds inside my chest. A curious, physical sensation, a humming of the sternum. I am part of this great, rumbling

US and now we're saying, " . . . and lead us not into temptation, but deliver us from evil . . . "

The Mass continues. We kneel, we line up and receive Communion, we kneel again and sit. And all through this my mind wanders . . . to the moon and back, to the warm sand at the beach, to the brittle pages of the book hidden under my bed.

Again we rise . . . But this is not part of the Mass. This is not when we usually stand. The priest has something to say to us. He's saying something about movies, about which movies we're allowed to go to. Am I hearing this right?

I whisper up to my father, "Is he talking about movies?"

But my father doesn't hear me, so intent is he on listening to what the priest is saying. I think, like me, he can't believe what he's hearing.

We are asked, all of us, to raise our right hands and say what the priest says. Obediently, I raise my hand, as everyone around us has done.

My parents are standing—but their hands remain defiantly at their sides. I pull *my* hand down and hide it behind my back.

Again, there's a rumbling all around us. But this time, I am no part of it. My parents, and I with them, remain silent as the rest of the flock vows to attend only those movies that are approved by the Church's Legion of Decency. I have no idea what a legion of decency might be. I do know that my parents are staring solemnly straight ahead, and my father's chest—right where his tie and lapels come together—is going in and out faster than usual, like he's trying to catch his breath.

And I know that this is important. My parents and I—my family together—have decided to separate ourselves, momentarily, from this flock.

It would be comforting to join in the mass recitation of these unexpected vows, to feel the low vibration resounding in our chests—massaging our hearts—to cooperate and be part of this *US*.

Instead, we stand together in our silence. The breeze has stiffened. It cools my burning face as the rhythmic chant of unforeseen vows surrounds, but does not overtake us. And I am as proud as I will ever be in my life to be a member of this tiny, rebellious congregation.

THANKSGIVING ABROAD,

1973

It's Thanksgiving morning. A low, lumpy sky spits rain into my face as I run to catch the train to the suburbs. I collapse into the seat, take a deep breath, close my eyes, and try to conjure up the smells that will saturate my mother's house today: apples, cinnamon, and that thick, welcoming smell of turkey innards and onions simmering on the stove.

Ingredients in our annual American Communion.

The train arrives at my stop and as I walk out into the street, the smell of diesel fumes reminds me that I am in France, and there will be no turkey feast today. In France it's just . . . Thursday. I hurry to the theatre where I meet my fellow junior-year-abroad American students. A director will lecture us about the play we saw here last weekend.

We gather in a meeting room right next to the auditorium, which is packed with noisy little kids. Luckily, when the door's closed, the hubbub disappears.

The director sweeps in. He's wearing a calf-length

leather coat and it swings freely from his shoulders, like a cape. He's a walking parody of an eccentric French man of the theatre, expounding on the play while pacing and gesturing hugely, pausing only to suck on the short cigarette held between his thumb and forefinger.

Keeping a straight face is not easy. But we make the effort; we try to pay attention. Someone is quietly passing around a big bag of M&M's. You can't get M&M's in France. They must be part of someone's care package from home. I hope there are some left by the time it reaches me.

And then it begins.

The soundtrack to–of all things–*The Wizard of Oz* comes bursting through the wall. There's no way we can pay attention to the French director now. It's hopeless.

I recognize the instrumental version of "Somewhere Over the Rainbow" and look around to see that we are all flicking tiny, discreet glances at our fellow countrymen, enjoying the shared surprise and recognition.

We continue to feign interest in what the director is saying to us, but the music is very loud, and I long to be on the other side of that wall, watching as Dorothy Gale of Kansas once again finds her way home.

All eyes are on the director as he pauses to light another cigarette. On the soundtrack, baby chicks are peeping.

Judy Garland begins her sweet, sad crooning of "Somewhere Over the Rainbow." Now, no one is looking at the director. We are not focusing on anything in that room as the soft shadow of homesickness settles on our faces.

Wordlessly, the bag is passed to me and I shake out a single M&M, a tan one, before I pass it along.

I pop it in my mouth and silently give thanks for this tiny feast.

THE DAWN'S EARLY LIGHT

It seems like every other day, some military official comes out and says, "Don't worry about this Y2K thing. Nuclear missiles can't get accidentally launched just because of a computer glitch."

Well, thanks for the reassurance, but now that the scenario has been planted in my brain, it's hard to stop thinking about it.

Worrying about this takes me back to the summer of 1974. I had figured that would be a good summer for a care-free tour of the islands of Greece. The Greeks thought it would be a good summer for a coup d'état and a little war with Turkey.

We were singing, the five of us, when the lights went out and people started running and screaming. The English kids had taught me the words to "What Shall We Do With a Drunken Sailor?" and we had just sung the line, "Ear-ly in the mor-nin'."

I was traveling alone that summer, but there was no shortage of English-speaking students to keep me company.

After a lingering supper at a restaurant under the stars,

and a few too many glasses of Retsina, we were sauntering down the taverna-lit main street of Malia, in Crete.

Just two days before, I had been sitting in a café, under a tree, watching a crowd of Greek men who'd gathered around a portable radio. An announcement came on, and their faces stiffened in concentration. When it was over, the men were pounding their fists on the table. Women came outside and they were crying. I asked a Greek girl what was going on. At five o'clock that morning, she said, Turkey attacked Cyprus and all the men between twenty-one and thirty-five would have to go into the army.

For the rest of that day, loudspeakers in the streets called out names and all the young men were taken away in buses.

Civilians were forbidden to travel. Rumors flashed through the tourist population: Turkey had napalmed Cyprus, Istanbul had been bombed, Turkish bombers were headed for Crete—for us.

Back in the café, I looked up through the branches as the dark wedge of a military plane passed over us.

Foreign radio signals were being jammed by the government. (By the way, there was a coup d'état in Athens in the middle of all this, but we didn't know about that yet.) And there were no newspapers.

We were already in the dark, so to speak, on that late evening when we had let the Retsina flow a little too freely, trying to anesthetize ourselves against fear.

We had left the restaurant in search of Ouzo when the loudspeakers blared out something in Greek, and people started running down the street and screaming. Then the lights went out and footsteps drummed past me in the blackness.

Someone called out, "Turkish bombers. They're headed this way!"

I walked back to my youth hostel and climbed the stairs to my bunk on the roof. I lay, staring up at the magnificent display of stars—a silvery bowl arching over me—listening hard for the hum of engines in the sky and wondering whether I'd ever see the sun again.

The next thing I knew, my face was hot with sunlight. Such a sweet awakening—ear-ly in the mor-nin'.

As it turned out, the war was contained in Cyprus. The announcement and the blackout were part of an air-raid drill. A few days later, I caught a jam-packed tourist boat back to Athens, and made my way back home.

It was nothing, really. A false alarm and panic. But the memory has stayed with me.

And now that there's talk about missiles being fired at us, due to incorrigible computers, on the eve of 2000, I pray that on the morning of January first, we will, all of us, have a sweet awakening.

Ear-ly in the morn-in'.

ÉCLAIR ENVY

There's this dream I've been having a few times a year for the past couple of decades. In it, I'm in Paris, and I'm trying to get to a bakery to get my hands on an éclair, but something always gets in my way.

I'll dream that I'm in a neighborhood that has no bakeries, or I'm in a bakery where I've been waiting in a long line, and when it's my turn, the clerk shakes his head and says it's closing time.

I know what you're thinking, and you can just cut it out right now. Look, sometimes, an éclair is just an éclair, and this is one of those times.

When I was in college, I spent a year in Paris. I was supposed to be studying at the Sorbonne, but if the truth be known, I spent a lot of time wandering the streets, going from bakery to bakery.

I would try to walk past without stopping, but one glance at a display of glistening ruby tarts, gossamer croissants and, of course, pale, delicate éclairs topped with chocolate frosting, and I would be drawn into that *pâtisserie* like I was hypnotized.

And that first bite—could anything compare with that? Smooth chocolate frosting yielding to buttery flakes of pastry, velvety cream filling made from sweet chocolate, heavy cream, and egg yolks.

When I came home to the United States, I'd come across a display of éclairs behind glass, and think: Maybe this one will be all right. Maybe someone at *this* bakery knows how an éclair *should* be made.

Hah. The recipe for real French éclairs must be classified information because American bakers don't seem to have a clue.

Grainy frosting, pastry with the taste and texture of cardboard, whitish-yellow filling that reeks of chemicals. What are they thinking? Do American bakers ever actually *taste* one of those things?

I try one every few years or so, whenever someone breathlessly informs me that there's a "great new bakery" in town.

These are the kind of bakeries that have those dry, pink cookies in the display case. And birthday cakes that are thin and flavorless and filmed with garish images of cartoon characters.

Who buys this stuff?

The people who recommend these bakeries are invariably the kind of people whose mothers baked from mixes and tucked Twinkies, Ho-Hos, and Ding-Dongs into their lunch boxes. People who like their brownies dry and cakey.

People who don't have a clue.

A few weeks ago, I was in the supermarket when I ran into a friend and told her about my latest éclair dream. In this one, I'm in Paris and I discover that there are *no* more bakeries *anywhere* in France.

They have become unfashionable.

My friend leaned in toward me and put her hand on my forearm. In a near-whisper she told me that there's this fabulous new bakery that just opened the other day, and guess what? they have éclairs.

I glanced down, and there was the face of Pocahontas staring up at me from the enormous sheet-cake lining the bottom of her shopping cart.

No wonder I have nightmares.

WET CRACKERS

I was seventeen years old, in the kitchen, mixing up a batch of brownies. I had just stirred in the walnuts and was happily spooning batter into my mouth—just to test it—when my mother sidled up to me and said, "Did I ever tell you about the wonderful dessert my mother used to make during the Depression?"

Ah, jeez, here we go: another Depression story. It was so hard to pay attention to grownups when they started in with these long-winded parables. And of course, there was a moral. Usually about how kids back then appreciated what they had.

"Okay," she said, "you take one package of common crackers—your grandmother called them Yankee crackers—and you split them in two."

Now, I'd had common crackers before, in clam chowder or something. They were big and tough and tasteless.

"Wait a minute," I said. "Crackers? I thought this was a dessert."

"I'm not finished. Look, this was the Depression—we didn't have chocolate and nuts. Those things cost a fortune. We were doing the best we could with what we had."

I was suspicious—like maybe this was all a joke—but I shut up and let her continue. While I was scraping the thick, chocolate batter from the saucepan into the brownie pan, Mum said, "So, you put the teakettle on . . . "

The teakettle? This did not sound auspicious.

"You put the teakettle on and meanwhile, arrange the split crackers on a big plate. Better yet, split enough for two big plates, otherwise people will be fighting over them."

Oh, right. This sounds like a scene straight out of *Oliver Twist.*

"You dot the crackers with butter—you don't need very much—and once the water's boiling, dribble a little bit of water on each of the crackers."

Wet crackers? Was she making this up? Cripes, I wished I had a witness!

I opened the oven and slid the pan in. If my mother hadn't been watching, I'd have scooped another little spoonful of batter out of the pan—just to even off the surface.

But she was right behind me, and now she was saying, "And, while they're still hot, you sprinkle a little bit of sugar over the tops of all the crackers."

"Okay . . . " I said, hoping that the next step would be to smother the whole mess with chocolate ice cream.

"That's it."

There was not a trace of sarcasm in her expression. She was dead serious.

"Okay, Mum, let me get this straight: You take wet crackers and sprinkle a little sugar on them . . . "

"Don't forget the butter . . . "

"Right, plus some butter . . . And your family actually *ate* this stuff?"

"Did we ever. We loved it."

The brownies baked, and I perched on the counter, inhaling the hot, chocolatey air drifting up from the oven. Hm. Wet crackers. . . . Maybe I was adopted.

Decades passed. Whenever I would get together with my sister and brother, we'd get so silly talking about Mum and her Depression treats that we'd end up doubled over, palming away tears. "Can you believe it?" someone always said.

Well, guess what? Those Yankee crackers that I figured were extinct are now available for fourteen bucks from some catalog. I did it: I sent away for a tin of them. And, while my kitchen filled up with the giggles and hoots and jeers coming from my three kids, I split those crackers, arranged them on a plate. I dotted and dribbled and sprinkled.

But, fool that I am, I only made one plateful . . . and we were fighting over them.

I swear.

A MAGIC PHONE

Last year, while visiting my mother, I was exploring boxes in her basement when I came across an old companion—the beige princess phone from our old house. I sat back on the cement floor, held it up and said, "Well, look at you!"

The numbers below the rotary dial were almost worn away from index fingers arcing along the same path for years, and the plastic housing on the base had a wide crack along the front, but this was it.

My sister and I would nearly kill ourselves trying to be the first one to get to this phone whenever it rang, leaping over chairs, clutter, each other, just in case the voice of a boy should be heard through those little holes in the round earpiece.

How sweet was the sound of a boy's voice on the other end, asking for me, our conversation elaborately casual as my heart pounded and I yanked the receiver into the bathroom, strangling the cord between the door and the jamb.

Through this heavy old receiver, I have spoken with my father. I have giggled with girlfriends, whispered with boyfriends. People long dead or long lost.

Alone in the musty gloom of my mother's cellar, I felt as

though I had discovered Aladdin's lamp. Maybe this was a magic telephone. On such a phone, you could contact the dead, the missing, the estranged. It would never be too late if you could find the right phone. Never too late for I'm sorry, or, I love you.

How sweet was the sound of a boy's
voice on the other end, asking for me . . .

There's a scene I watched, years ago, in the movie *Peggy Sue Got Married*, where Kathleen Turner travels back in time to her teenaged years. She answers the phone and hears the voice of her long-dead grandmother. That scene was unbearably poignant. My throat constricted painfully and I was practically gasping by the time their conversation was over.

It set me to wondering about our old phone. Wondering whatever happened to it, wondering whether reality might just dissolve for a moment, if only I could lay hands on that phone again.

And so, feeling foolish, and hoping I wouldn't be caught, I lifted the receiver to my ear and made a wish: That I could hear the voice of my father.

What I found was not the expansive silence of a working phone, with the sound of my breathing circulating up and out the earpiece. What I found was dead silence.

Ah, well . . .

PART TWO

BUTTERSCOTCH, VELVET THRONES, AND BOYD TINSLEY'S BRAIDS

AN ODE TO
SCOTT SIMON

It's Saturday morning. My eyes are still closed when I hear a voice. Am I dreaming? No, it's Scott Simon. I'm too sleepy to know what he's saying, but that voice—that *butterscotch* voice. Oh, he's telling me what's been happening in the world. Without shouting. Without sound bites. Without sensationalism. He's explaining to me, so patiently, what's happening in Ireland.

And now, as I drift back into sleep, Scott is reading to me from a children's story book.

. . . I'm in love with Scott Simon. There. I've said it. I can't hold onto this secret any longer.

I didn't always feel this way. Time was, I could listen to him with an intellectual appreciation. Enjoy his sense of humor. (Don't you love the way he laughs? It's midway between a guffaw and a chortle. I can just see him trying to control himself, stifling laughter, maybe turning off his microphone to have a good belly laugh.)

No, I didn't always feel this way. The turning point came during the Gulf War. One day, a different announcer took his place. He said that Scott was on assignment in Saudi Arabia.

Saudi Arabia? I panicked. What were they thinking, sending such a gentle soul into a war zone? He could get hurt. He could get killed.

Then, a few days later, he filed a report from Saudi Arabia. He had witnessed an attack by a scud missile. This is how his report began: "The sky screamed, and the ground barked . . . "

Ohh . . . *that's* why they sent him. Because he can *write.* He can write in a way that makes us feel as though we are right there with him, witnessing with him, through him.

You can push those buttons on your radio until your finger is sore, but you won't find anything else on your'dial that comes anywhere close to this stuff. Am I right?

I have this recurring nightmare—that I wake up one Saturday morning, my radio turns itself on, and all I hear is static. My Public Radio station has disappeared from the airwaves.

I'll be straight with you—I cannot live without Scott Simon. I've got to hear that intelligent, sincere, *butterscotch* voice once a week.

Is that so much to ask?

All I want you to do is pick up the phone, call the station and say, "Yes, doggone it. I want to help those two crazy kids keep in touch."

Thank you.

VIRGINIA FESTIVAL OF

THE BOOK, 1999

Every spring in Charlottesville, Virginia, something terrific happens.

There's this festival. And it's not a festival that honors watermelons or monster trucks. This festival honors The Book.

For four days, this town is crawling with all kinds of writers and publishers, editors, critics, and literary agents. They come here from all over just so they can talk to us—and maybe sell us a few autographed books. Crammed into those four days are more than a hundred-and-fifty programs. Some for children, lots for grownups, and all for people who love books.

This is the Virginia Festival of the Book.

***

I trotted happily from one venue to the next.

Sharon McCrumb told us a true story from the 1800s about

a man who was murdered and then was buried under three separate headstones. Now *there's* an image that'll stick with you.

For those of us with unpublished manuscripts, these authors give us hope. If we keep at it, then one day we may be up in front of everyone, reading aloud from our hefty books, advising and inspiring other wannabes.

My favorite panel, every year, is the one that features literary agents. It's held at Charlottesville's City Council chambers. The four agents were seated way above us, like Supreme Court justices, or the Wizard of Oz. They made their pronouncements from on high, and we—the great unpublished—hung on their every word.

The piece of advice that makes me laugh, every year, is that the unpublished writer should approach several agents, and interview them all to decide which agency to go with. What a hoot.

Agents are flooded with letters from unpublished writers. They don't even want to look at your manuscript, forget about representing you.

This is like advising someone on how to marry a millionaire. Okay, approach several millionaires, interview them, and decide which one you want to marry. As if!

***

This was the fifth year of the festival. In years past I've sat at the back of these conference rooms, along with my friend, Avery. He's a writer, too. We were like the kids at the back of the classroom, passing notes and sizing up the panelists. Afterwards, we'd introduce ourselves to the speakers. You could call that networking. I call it the art of the power-schmooze. You never know who might connect you to the right literary agent, or the right publisher.

Well, this year, Avery's had his first book published, so he was one of the panelists.

This time around, even *I* got to be on a panel. An essay of mine was published in an anthology and eight of the writers were invited to come to the festival and read. I wondered who'd show up and listen to *us*, especially when Rita Dove was reading her poetry someplace else at the same time.

Well, *seven* people showed up to listen to us. And all but one of them was related to one of the writers. But it was fun to wear a name tag and be on a panel. We took turns reading out loud. And afterwards we signed each other's books.

There were big name authors at the Festival, too. David Baldacci, Sharon McCrumb, and Alice McDermott. Rita Dove. No way were all those people crammed into the Culbreth Theatre related to them.

***

There was a 500-person luncheon at the Omni Hotel. Alice McDermott was the guest of honor.

I couldn't swing the twenty-five dollar ticket to the luncheon, but I wanted to listen to her speech, so they let me stand up in the back of the room–and it was packed. I was squeezed in next to a busing station. From what I could see on the plates next to me, it was a pretty good lunch. I think it was salmon.

Now, I should have eaten lunch before I got there. I don't know what I was thinking. But somewhere in the middle of Alice McDermott's speech, I thought I would faint from hunger and from standing in one spot for so long.

The subject of her speech was Books That Changed My Life. She told us that books don't actually alter the course of your life—after all, you're born, you pay taxes, and you die whether or not you ever made it all the way through *Ulysses*—but they change how you *perceive* your life. At least, I think that was the gist of her speech. I was really hungry.

Earlier, I had watched as people poured into the function room. The guest of honor was the last to go in, accompanied by a gaggle of starry-eyed companions. I love this. Because, during an earlier presentation, Alice McDermott told us that she's a housewife and mother who does her writing after she takes the kids to school and decides what house-cleaning to put off in order to get a few pages written.

***

On the last night of the festival, there was a wing-ding held at Carr's Hill, home of the University of Virginia's president, John Casteen. Harry and I had a very good time, what with all the food and wine. John Casteen didn't appear to be home and I don't know what was up with that. If there was a party at my house, you can bet I'd be there.

But it was fun to get together with all the people we'd seen on the panels over the past few days. Only here, they no longer behaved like agents or editors or famous writers. Everyone was friendly and accessible. Sipping wine and laughing.

I'm telling you, the opportunities for power-schmoozes were head-spinning.

***

For me, the best part of this festival was after I read my little essay aloud—when I heard the applause. People listened and they laughed and they clapped. All seven of them. It was great. How wonderful for a writer to hear applause.

And this is what's so terrific about the festival. It's called the Festival of the Book, but a book is an author's voice in print. This is a festival of the author. It honors people who write things down, people who tell stories.

In daily life, most writers are not even honored with so much as a paycheck. My children think that Mum has this embarrassing hobby, as though writing essays and novels is like making jewelry out of macaroni or using decoupage to paper the walls.

***

But once a year, for four days—right here in Charlottesville—there's a coming together of writers and readers. What a great idea.

By the way, if you like this essay, when it's over, could you applaud? Just this once.

Thanks.

A NIGHT

AT THE OPERA

Every Saturday, when I was a kid, my mother would tune our tinny kitchen radio to Texaco's Metropolitan Opera presentation. She dusted or cooked as she hummed along.

I didn't get it. I would watch her and shake my head. I couldn't understand her fascination with faraway singers bellowing in a foreign language.

Years later, I was a college student in Paris. I had been there for four months when my sister—and my mother— came to visit me.

On Christmas Eve, the three of us trooped out into the drizzly darkness, headed for the opera house and a performance of *La Bohème*.

We found our seats down front—they were like thrones. Velvet with gold-painted wood trim. And they didn't fold up.

Then, the music began. This was not the kind of music that funnels through a pair of speakers. This music was ev-

erywhere. Surely, this is what heaven sounds like, with its
never-before-seen colors and never-before-heard sounds: The
orchestra, now soothing, now stirring, Mimi and Rodolfo singing different words at the same time, and it all sounded so
perfect and then at the end of that song they both sang *amor*
at the same time and held the note forever.

I was no passive spectator to this. I was included in this
miracle, my own heart soaring with Mimi's new love.

As the evening passed, life became more complicated
for Mimi and Rodolfo. Mimi was sick, coughing, like she had
tuberculosis or something. Still, she sang like an angel. Near
the end, Mimi was lying in bed, still singing away, but weaker
and weaker.

The music was so beautiful, so optimistic . . . American,
almost. It was impossible to think the ending could be anything but happy. I wished *my* whole life could be orches-
trated like this, with violins whimpering during my sad times
and a full orchestra, with trumpets, rejoicing along with my
high-spirited moments.

And then—unbelievably—Mimi sang one last note, and
she *died*. It felt like a trick. She was so young. What was Puccini
thinking? This was much too sad. Tears welled up in my eyes
and I had a lump in my throat that could not be massaged
away with a swallow.

As the performers took their bows, all I could think was:
I'd better pull myself together before the lights come up.
Embarrassing to be found sobbing over some opera.

Even now, when I cook or dust while listening to my
kitchen radio as a faraway performance of *La Bohème* funnels
through the speakers, that same feeling of optimism overtakes me and I still hold out the foolish hope that this time—
maybe this time—Mimi will make it.

And as the music floats toward a thundering close, I find
myself wiping away tears and sniffling.

My daughter watches me, and she doesn't get it. She

wants to know: How can I care so much about this stuff I'm hearing on the radio? Who cares about faraway singers bellowing in a foreign language?

I can't wait to take her to Paris.

GIVE US MONEY

My niece, Jennifer, just got married. Lovely ceremony, tons of relatives.

I'm standing out in front of the church, blowing bubbles at the bride and groom, when I catch a glimpse of a guy I'd call a tangential relative. The second husband of a sister of an in-law. I'd seen him in the church and hadn't even bothered to say hello.

More than once, I've sat at a Thanksgiving or Easter dinner table with him, but to tell you the truth, I never really cared for the guy. No reason, really. I just never bothered to get to know him and I figured we had nothing in common.

We all head for the parking lot. As we're getting into our cars to go to the reception, I notice, on the rear bumper of this man's car, a small, tasteful bumper sticker.

A Public Radio bumper sticker.

Well, well.

Of course, I sought him out at the reception, and while everyone else was doing the Chicken Dance and the Macarena, the two of us discovered that we had quite a lot in common.

Neither of us is interested in car mechanics, but we both

get a good laugh listening to "Car Talk." We're both immensely grateful that Daniel Schorr has not retired. And, to my surprise, we had both heard, and tried, the recipe for NPR chicken—a recipe that was broadcast on "All Things Considered." (You somehow cook a two-pound chicken for a mere 35 minutes, and it involves a whole lot of salt, as I recall. It came out great.)

We are not a secret society; we are a subtle society.

This conversation confirmed what I'd known all along: That NPR listeners are an interesting and interested collection of people. Although we come from all walks of life—kindergarten teachers, housewives, large animal veterinarians—we can be identified by our small, tasteful bumper stickers, our coffee mugs, and tote bags.

We are not a secret society; we are a subtle society.

You have to *look* for the signs. But do look for them, *identify* the other intelligent and well-informed people that cross your path.

You are not alone.

So, when you see someone using, say, a Public Radio pen, or sipping from a Public Radio mug, with a raise of your eyebrows and an upward nod of your chin, say, "NPR?" You will have found a kindred soul.

Maybe you're thinking: But *I* don't have a Public Radio bumper sticker or a Public Radio pen, or totebag! How will *I* be recognized?

You know, don't you, what you have to do, right now.

MOVIE MARATHON

I am a lucky duck. Why? Because I live near Charlottesville, Virginia. And every year, around Halloween, the Virginia Film Festival comes to town. I don't have to go anywhere. I don't have to take a plane or find a hotel; this festival comes to *me*.

This year, I got to go to the opening gala held at the Bayly Art Museum. Tickets are forty bucks a pop for the gala, but if you go, you just might spot the Hollywood big shots who've been invited to the festival. My husband won a pair of tickets to the gala from a radio station, so we got to see how the other half lives—for a few hours, anyway.

You're supposed to get dressed up for this opening night wing-ding, so I dug out my one pair of high heels from the back of my closet. I thought I looked pretty cute in my heels and black minidress until I got there and saw all those young, willowy blondes. Oh, well. I don't know where *they* came from.

After a visit to the wine bar, we headed straight for the food table, where we were not disappointed. There was an entire salmon encrusted with mustard seeds. And, there were duck strips to be dipped in chutney. Kind of like a

trip to Chik-Fil-A, but with a better class of poultry and deluxe dip.

We milled around looking for famous people and found *other* people milling around looking for famous people. I stepped out onto the front porch to watch Rip Torn being interviewed under a blinding television light.

As we watched the interview, we struck up a conversation with a woman who'd come to the festival from Washington, DC. She looked pretty normal—she was fiftyish, had a New York accent—but there was something a little creepy about her. I couldn't put my finger on what it was, until we got to talking about famous people and she confided that she had once stalked the Dalai Lama. I don't think there was anything sinister about it, but she stalked him, nonetheless, over the course of several days. I didn't dare tell her that the Dalai Lama would be visiting Charlottesville the following week.

I bet that would make a good movie: *Stalking the Dalai Lama.*

Pretty soon, Rip Torn walked up the steps to the entrance of the museum. As he passed me, he smiled and said, "Hi." I considered telling him that I remembered him in *Ben Casey,* but I figured he probably remembered that, too, so what was the point?

We left the gala early, because we were due at the Regal Cinema on the downtown mall to see *Blowup.* That's the Antonioni movie from the '60s that's like *Austin Powers,* only serious.

I wasn't happy about leaving the gala while there was still wine and salmon left, but, after all, that's the point of the festival: movies.

And there were movies: old movies, new movies, experimental movies, classic movies. And people who *know* about movies and *make* movies come to Charlottesville (*they* take the planes and find the hotels) to fill us in on what went into making all those movies.

***

Over the next three days, I sprinted from one movie to the next. They were showing at three theatres in Charlottesville: The Regal Cinema, Vinegar Hill Theatre, and Culbreth Theatre. There was no time for meals, so I'd grab a Snickers bar from CVS and eat it while jogging toward the next venue. Someone with ready-made sandwiches and a pushcart could make a fortune during the film festival.

One of the movies I saw was *The Manchurian Candidate.* Early '60s, Frank Sinatra, military brainwashing, assassination. . . . It was great. And afterward, David Amram—who composed the music for the movie—spoke to us and answered questions. He told us that it came out shortly before JFK's assassination, and it was withdrawn right after the shooting, because the parallels were too disturbing.

On Friday, my husband, daughter, and I went to the Culbreth Theatre to watch an evening of Charlie Chaplin movies, three short ones. I'd never been as impressed with his movies as I figured I was supposed to be, plus I'd really only seen snippets of them on TV.

But, at the Festival, there was a live, ragtime orchestra providing musical accompaniment to the movies, and sound effects, too. It was wonderful. The place was packed, and everyone was laughing.

The next time I went to the Culbreth Theatre, it was packed again, and again everyone was in stitches, but the movie wasn't Charlie Chaplin's—it wasn't even a comedy. It was James Dean in *Rebel Without A Cause.*

It was funny in the same way that *Airplane* is funny—as a send-up of the genre. Jim Backus had the Leslie Neilson role. In one scene, we were supposed to understand that Jim Backus was a hen-pecked husband. So, he was wearing a frilly, lace-trimmed apron, but not just over a shirt—he was wear-

ing the apron over a suit and tie. That's just one example.
This movie was a riot.

***

The best part, every year, of the Film Festival is the three-day,
six-hour, shot-by-shot analysis of a movie.

This year, Roger Ebert was back to walk us through
Antonioni's *Blowup*. After a few minutes of opening remarks
in front of the crowd, he takes a seat in the darkened theatre,
wearing a microphone and holding a remote control for the
video-disc machine, so he can stop and start the film, go
backward or forward.

From his seat, he makes comments about the movie: how
it was made, some background about the director, stories
about the actors, or what the director is trying to accomplish
by using a particular shot or camera angle.

The other element in this process is what Ebert calls,
"democracy in the dark." Anyone in the theatre can call out a
comment or question. In *Blowup*, people called out remarks
about all the red-painted buildings and red cars that
Antonioni included in his scenes of London.

One man in the audience remarked, more than a few
times, on a photograph hanging on a wall next to the pro-
tagonist. The photograph looked to be a star, maybe the sun,
surrounded by blackness. This guy kept calling out comments about the picture of the *eclipse* on the wall. Clearly, this
was not an eclipse—it was the antithesis of an eclipse. There
was no black disc in the middle, nothing obscuring the light.
But this guy would not let it go. Lucky for him *we* were in
darkness, and he was effectively anonymous; otherwise he
would never live this down.

That's what Roger Ebert means by "democracy in the
dark." Anyone can say anything.

Telling that story makes me feel smug, like I'm so smart

because I know what an eclipse looks like. So now, I have a confession to make.

A few years ago, the movie we were analyzing was *The Third Man*. That's that moody, *film noir* from the late 1940s with Joseph Cotten and Orson Welles. At one point, I called out what I thought was a straightforward, intelligent question. I spoke up nice and loud, so everyone could hear me, and said, "So, who was the third man?" In case you're not familiar with this movie, let me tell you, this is the single, dumbest question ever posed during one of these shot-by-shot sessions. Until now, nobody knew who the idiot was.

***

The last movie I went to, on Sunday afternoon, was *Shadrach*. It's based on a short story by William Styron, and the filmmaker was his daughter, Susanna Styron. I thought it was a lovely movie. Andie MacDowell is in it—you know, the gorgeous Andie MacDowell—and the character she plays does *not* have a flat stomach. Her stomach is soft and round, the way it's supposed to be after you've given birth a few times. That sight alone was worth the seven-dollar ticket price.

It's the story, told through the perceptions of a little white boy, of a ninety-nine-year-old former slave who has returned to what used to be the plantation where he grew up, in order to die, and be buried there.

When it was over, both Susanna and William Styron appeared in person to discuss the movie. The audience was infested with graduate students and academic types who were very unhappy with William Styron because he didn't tell *their* stories, he told *his* story. These academics were looking for an exhaustive dissertation on slavery and its ramifications. They were disappointed because what they got was a good story, well told.

And that was the 1998 Virginia Film Festival. Lots of

movies, lots of opinions. God bless America.

I went home and had my first real meal in three days, then collapsed into bed, exhausted, my head spinning with images from other people's imaginations.

It was great.

JOURNEY TO
THE EAST

We're late. My son, Waldo, and I were stuck in the kind of traffic jam that is so monstrous it makes you examine your conscience, trying to figure out what trespass you have committed to deserve frustration of this magnitude.

But we made it, and now we're at the Virginia Beach amphitheater.

Already, we've missed the opening act, and as I thread my way among the firm bodies of the high school and college crowd, I'm a sweaty, frizzy-haired old broad who's wondering why she has sat in a car on a one-hundred-degree day for five hours in order to arrive at this rock concert.

I remind myself that I'm not doing this for my son—he could've driven here by himself. I'm doing it for *me*, because I'm a fan of the Dave Matthews Band.

Just as I'm wishing I'd brought a towel to mop up my prolific sweat, the music starts.

As each song begins I hear the first couple of notes and I know what song it is. My heart rises and swells as I'm hit with wave after wave of joyous recognition and as the music surges I'm swept up and carried away and I'm singing along and loving it—loving being right here, right now:

Watching Boyd Tinsley, live, in front of me, assaulting his violin like a madman, his braids whipping through the air over his head.

Witnessing Dave Matthews as he pumps that left knee up and down—just like I saw him do on *Saturday Night Live*—as he alternately growls and purrs into the microphone.

And the spellbinding light show: greens and purples and reds and blues, pulsating and waving with the music.

And at this moment I am ageless, timeless, drawn out of myself and into the music.

Dave Matthews performing in my front yard
—that would be very cool.

Then, abruptly, this tidal wave of music that has buoyed me up for three hours tosses me back down on shore.

Oh, right. I'm at Virginia Beach, and once again I'm an old broad among tender youth. We shuffle out along the wide path that curves around the amphitheater, suffocating in the heat and the crowd, like pilgrims at Mecca making a slow swing around the *Kaaba*.

Waldo and I scuttle back to the far reaches of the sandy parking lot and begin the journey back to Charlottesville.

And now: the traffic, the humidity, the heat, that awful tunnel, hours more on the interstate.

I know what you're thinking: Was it worth it?

Well, to the Moslem who journeys to Mecca; is it worth it?

To the pilgrim who *walked* to Canterbury; was it worth it?

To the football fan who travels to the Superbowl; is *that* worth it?

Look at it this way: It was worth sitting in a sweltering amphitheater for *three* hours in order to spend *ten* hours in the car with my son.

What I've discovered from driving my kids around these last twenty years is that only small segments of my life consist of *here* or *there*. Much of the time is spent in between. And yes, I complain sometimes, but the truth is that I've come to enjoy and appreciate the in-betweens.

Is it worth it? You bet.

Which is not to say that I would be averse to Dave Matthews performing in my front yard—that would be very cool.

SWING DANCE

Rock step. Right, left. Rock step.

Look at me, I'm dancing! I'm swing dancing. Just like my fifteen-year-old daughter, just like my eighty-year-old mother. It seemed like everyone but me knew how to swing dance, so my husband and I signed up for a parks and rec. course in East Coast Swing Dancing.

And now, it's hard to stop. Even when I'm by myself, standing at the stove, stirring the soup, or waiting in line at the supermarket checkout, I find myself stepping backward with my right foot, then side to side, whispering, "rock step, right, left, rock step." Or maybe, "rock step, step, *turn*, rock step." I've been learning tricky stuff like that. Inside turns, tuck turns, belt wraps.

When Harry and I were engaged and in our early twenties, we took a class in ballroom dancing. The gymnasium was filled with ancient, middle-aged people brushing up on the fox trot and the waltz.

We took the class because we figured it would be a kind of campy, hokey fun. The whippersnappers were gonna show the old folks how good we could be.

Well, we were pathetic. Or I was, anyway. I just could not get the hang of sequential steps. This course went on for twelve weeks and I never learned even one dance.

Right after the course ended, we got married. There's a picture someone took at our wedding, of our first dance together. In it, I'm looking down at my feet, mouthing, "One two three, one two three," and the guests are standing all around us, laughing.

Very seldom in the twenty-two years following our wedding have I attempted to dance. I did take a ballet course once, but the whole experience had an *I Love Lucy* quality about it. When all the other dancers were going *this* way, I was going *that* way. The only thing missing was the laugh track.

Years later, I discovered that one of my sons had Attention Deficit Disorder, and I was pretty sure that I had it, too. Among the signs of ADD are disorganization, impulsivity, and uh . . . oh, I can never remember the third thing. . . .

Short term memory loss, that's it. Anyway, a symptom of the disorganization is a serious problem with sequencing.

People with ADD are the kind of people who can't mow the lawn in straight lines. We feel compelled to write our names in the grass with the mower. We don't go from a to b to c, we go from a to q to f. . . .

One day, I glanced at a photograph on my mantel. I'd looked at this photo hundreds of times before. It's a picture of my daughter putting on a ballet slipper before a recital. This time, when I looked at the picture, a lightning bolt hit me: Aha! Sequencing. That's why I can't learn dance steps.

Well, about a year ago, I finally got help for my own ADD problems. My doctor prescribed Wellbutrin, one of the drugs that work for ADD. Twice a day I take the purple pill with the one-eyed happy-face on it, and now, I can finish things that I start, I can refrain from interrupting people, and, best of all, I can dance.

Watch me.

RADIO REDEMPTION

It's Christmas Eve, and I've had it. I've had it with the tacky decorations in the suffocating, overheated stores I've been trapped in. I've had it with tasteless Christmas ditties on rock stations. I've had it with worries about who gets what gift and how are we gonna pay for all this stuff anyway?

Right after Thanksgiving, I start to vibrate at a higher rate. My heart races into December, my mind swirling with to-do lists: stuff to cook, stuff to buy, stuff to wrap, stuff to hide.

And always, in the back of my mind, is the fear that I'm forgetting something essential. Did I forget to buy a present for somebody? Is there someplace I'm supposed to be right now? And I fear that the spiritual heart of Christmas has been completely obscured in all these preparations—and in my life. I'm afraid that I'm doing it all wrong. Everything.

Then, every Christmas Eve, just as I fear I will implode from the pressures of the material world, I hear a voice—it's coming from my radio. " . . . from the historic chapel of King's College in Cambridge, England, *A Festival of Nine Lessons and Carols.*"

I turn up the radio, sit back, and take a deep breath. Oh,

right. It's Christmas Eve. I've done all I can do—or all I'm gonna do, anyway. This is the finish line.

The lone choir boy, his voice high and hypnotic, sings those first, haunting, notes of, "Once in Royal David's City," and every muscle in my body abandons the chase and relaxes.

The familiar Bible passages are soothing, reassuring, like hearing your mother read, *Good Night, Moon*, for the hundredth time. Only what I'm hearing now is, "Fear not, for behold, I bring you good tidings of great joy, which shall be to all people."

I could listen to *that* every night.

The choir starts in on that ancient carol, "Adam Lay Ybounden," with harmonies so intricate and delicate they break your heart. Music so gorgeous, I inhale it, savor it, hoping to capture this moment and hold onto it forever.

By the time they get to, "Oh, Come All Ye Faithful," hot tears are sliding down my cheeks. Why? How is it that happiness and relief bring tears?

I don't want this to end. I'd like to curl up and take a vacation inside my soul.

The final notes of the final song, "Hark, the Herald Angels Sing," fade into silence. And for the first time in weeks, I am calm, my breaths come slow and deep.

The whirlwind planning is over. For the next thirty hours or so, I will live in the moment: Be here now.

A space has been cleared. In this space I will remember who I am, remember why I'm here.

And, best of all, I will remember to fear not.

FALLING ASLEEP

IN ALL THE WRONG PLACES

I am not my husband. My husband is not me.

I silently repeat this mantra over and over as I sit next to Harry at a poetry reading. We are seated in the front row—part of a small, cozy audience. The poet is a friend of mine, Cathryn Hankla, and she's very good. Cathy's reading a lively, funny prose poem. I sneak a sideways glance at Harry and see that his eyes are closed and his mouth is open. He's asleep.

Did I mention that we're sitting in the front row?

I picked up a copy of Cathy's new book, and have placed it strategically on my knee. It's a slim paperback, so it has nice, sharp edges. Every time I see Harry's eyelids flutter—which is something like every twenty seconds—under cover of my hand, I press my knee in his direction and give him a discreet jab to the thigh with the corner of the poetry book.

His eyelids slap open like window shades. He smiles a

little and gives the appearance of someone who's paying attention—for about fifteen seconds, anyway.

Then we repeat the cycle.

If you've ever brought a three-year-old to church, you know how exhausting it is to be constantly focused on this person next to you, trying hard to pre-empt any reason for him to call attention to himself and bring embarrassment upon you both.

Well, this is the story of my life, because my husband has a real talent for sleeping. In any situation that doesn't call for his direct participation, his brain shifts into "audience" mode, and then goes dormant.

At the end of movies, he walks out shaking his head, complaining that the plot "lacked continuity."

Well, yeah, if you slept through the second act.

Movies, operas, concerts . . . And they don't even have to turn out the lights. His brain snaps right into audience mode the minute the program begins. Then, as if on cue from a post-hypnotic suggestion, his head starts bobbing, and those eyelids begin their halting, but inevitable, descent.

One time, he and just *two* other parents were invited to observe my son's dance class. Bright lights, loud music, little kids dancing all around him—and Harry's slumped in the metal folding chair with his chin on his chest.

I am a lunatic to have taken my husband to a poetry reading. I don't know what I was thinking. But I figured that sitting a mere four feet in front of the poet—an uncommonly pretty, young poet—that that'd keep him awake.

Hah.

I should probably just let him sleep, if that's what he wants to do. After all, it's him, not me. I should stop caring.

I am not my husband, and my husband is not me.

Right?
Oh, Cathy, I am so sorry.

***

Cathryn Hankla's sharp little book of prose poems is called The
Texas School Book Depository.

PART THREE

WHERE THE HOLY PEOPLE GROW

I never knew a groundhog could laugh . . .

A REVOLTING

DEVELOPMENT

My doctor's appointment is in four minutes. I'm sitting in my car, my thumbs twitching against the steering wheel, wondering when traffic will start moving again.

Great, now we're rolling, but why so slow? I'm not on a highway. I'm not in a city. I'm not even in the suburbs. I'm on a road in the country.

Where did all these cars come from? Where did all these *people* come from? And it gets worse every day. When I moved here six years ago, I could stop my car in the middle of this road and look at the mountains for a minute or two, and *no* one would come up behind me.

That's six years ago, not sixty.

Now, I like to think of myself as a kind, reasonable person, but this self-image has been put to the test lately by a villain. That villain is: The *Developer*.

Like Jerry Seinfeld saying, "*Newman*," that word is uttered with disdain among *my* family and friends.

Developer.

I have no problem with builders who put up a house here, a house there, especially when the impact on the surrounding land is minimal.

The real villain, the Snidely Whiplash of rural America, is the developer who comes in with bulldozers and destroys a tract of graceful, picturesque landscape, replacing our beautiful countryside with dozens—sometimes hundreds—of houses.

This morning, I'm rolling along at five miles an hour past a bright green field dotted with cows the color of heavy cream. Butterflies dance around blue cornflowers at the edge of the road. And I wonder: How soon will it be before these cows are evicted, the rolling field flattened, all of this replaced by acres of aluminum and vinyl boxes, a checkerboard of little yards saturated with herbicides and insecticides, where no butterfly will survive?

And every house has at least two cars.

Sitting in traffic and thinking about developers is an unhealthy combination. My blood pressure must be through the roof. I tell myself: Breathe deeply, relax those shoulders. Think of this as a lazy tour of the countryside.

And think of the developer. He has a family to feed. Maybe kids in college. And this is how he makes his living. Who are you to tell this guy he can't feed his family? He means no harm.

This is where my internal dialogue heats up.

Okay, I understand that he means no harm. Just like the termites that are destroying the floor under your feet. *They* mean no harm. It's not personal. They're just very good at what they do.

We're moving faster now. Twenty-seven miles an hour. The woman behind me, in the black Suburban, is tailgating so close, she's practically in my back seat. If I wanted to be this close to strangers, I would've moved to New York.

My question for the developer is this: How will you know when you're done? Will it be when every farm and forest and meadow is covered with houses and stores and asphalt? And what will you do then? What will you do once you've ruined everything? If the answer is, "Go someplace else." Why don't you go there now?

Right now. Just don't go by car, because you'd never get out of here. Take a plane, take a helicopter.

Take a hike.

GUERILLA GROUNDHOG

I was relaxing on the porch, admiring my husband's garden fortress, when I spied the intruder . . . and my heart froze.

We moved to the country because we'd had it with crime and stress. Here, we were one with nature. Here, we had found Paradise.

And then Harry had to go and plant a garden.

I knew our paradise days were over when Harry stormed into the house holding a gorgeous eggplant—with a bite taken out of it. He held up the defiled eggplant, and I think there were tears in his eyes as he said, "Groundhog."

From then on, Harry's groundhog would waddle out to the garden every day and gorge on the best all-you-can-eat salad bar he'd ever seen.

Harry tried throwing rocks at him, but kept missing.

It was time for a fence: some lightweight chicken wire and metal posts.

I never knew a groundhog could laugh, but the morning after that fence went up, I swear I heard this one chuckle. He flattened that fence and chomped the lettuce plants down to stubs.

Time for a serious fence: four-by-four posts, two-by-four railings, a trench a foot and a half deep all around the perimeter in which to bury the base of the chicken wire. Now, the groundhog can't burrow under and he can't jump over.

Every day, Harry checked on the state of the fence and its industrial-strength chicken wire. No holes: A perfect fortress. Lettuce flourished, tomatoes ripened. It was great.

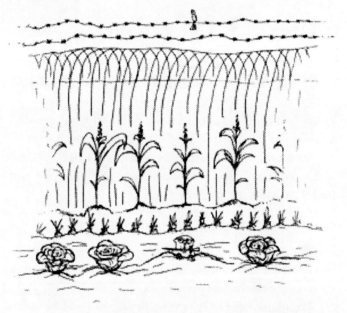

He vaulted over the top—like he was made for this kind of thing.

Until that day when I was sitting on the porch, and saw our fat marauder happily munching his way through the tender leaves in Harry's lettuce patch. I jumped up, stamped my feet, and hollered, "Get lost, you . . . "

Well, I can't tell you exactly what I said, but "son of a gun" will do for now.

So I'm screaming, "Get out of here, you . . . son of a gun"

and I can only imagine what the neighbors thought was going on over at our house.

Turns out, our lumbering pirate can really move. He turned and looked at me, like—who was I to be yelling at him? Then shot over the strawberries and up to the fence. Then, like one of those nimble gang members in *West Side Story*, he scrambled up the wire fence and vaulted over the top, like he was made for this kind of thing.

This spring, Harry has been hard at work planning his garden—has it all mapped out on a piece of paper. Little squares labeled, "butter lettuce, green beans, strawberries."

He might as well take his little garden map and give it to the groundhog for a menu. There's no keeping out that groundhog.

But Harry has a plan: Right now, he's out there extending the chicken wire so it goes up higher than the fence and sort of curves over backward toward the outside of the enclosure.

The groundhog will climb up and wonder how come he's upside down just before he falls off. He'll never get over that fence.

Well, we'll see. I bet that rascal's peering over the edge of his hole right now, watching Harry and snickering.

POSSESSION—WITH INTENT TO DISTRIBUTE

I've just come from the health food store, and now I'm singing along with the radio and tapping my thumbs on the steering wheel. I slide the sun roof open to let in some cool night air. Glancing up into my rear view mirror, I notice the police car in the distance behind me. No lights revolving or anything, he's just behind me.

Now, I'm merely humming, as my mind leaps back to a conversation I had with a friend a few weeks ago. She told me that there's this bill making its way through the State House in Richmond. A bill that would make it a crime to possess any substance whatsoever that resembles a controlled substance, *if* there's a likelihood that it could be mistaken for a controlled substance.

Notice that it's not if you're trying to *pass it off* as a controlled substance, only if it's likely that someone could *mistake* it for a controlled substance.

I stop humming and think about the grocery bag in my

back seat. At the health food store, I bought a bunch of stuff in bulk. There's oregano in a Baggy, sage in a Baggy . . . and what else? Oh, who cares. That's enough.

I glance into the mirror again and the squad car is closer. I have gone into a whole-body cringe: my stomach, my lungs, my face . . . Do I have a taillight that's burned out? What about that little light over the license plate? I never think to check stuff like that. What if I get pulled over? What if the cop glances into the back seat and sees my stash of suspicious Baggies?

I don't even have the receipt. Just the lookalike spices in my cloth carry-bag.

I pray that Heloise herself will be my expert witness . . .

And now, I remember something else that's in my car. Now, I'm lightheaded, and a wave of nausea overtakes me.

We bought this Volvo used. Nice car, good price, but it smelled like a hamster cage. No problem, I'd said to my husband, not for nothing have I been reading *Hints from Heloise* these past thirty years.

We bought the car, driving it away in *February* with the windows rolled down. That's how bad the smell was. Back home, I got out my trusty box of baking soda. I blanketed the car with that stuff. The seats, the carpet, the dashboard, the trunk. Later, I vacuumed it all up but there was still some residual stink, so I opened both the ashtrays and filled them with baking soda.

And I never emptied them.

AQU

Oh, my God.

In my panic I let up on the gas pedal, and now the cop's on my tail. Any second now, the spinning blue light will reflect into my eyes.

The coming scenario flashes through my mind: Me, led away in handcuffs. And the headline in the newspaper tomorrow: HOUSEWIFE BUSTED FOR COCAINE AND MARIJUANA. And my trial: I pray that Heloise herself will be my expert witness for the cocaine part of it, swearing under oath that, yes indeed, she has recommended that her readers *simply* fill their ashtrays with baking soda in order to banish unpleasant odors in the car.

And then it happens. There's a silent burst of blue light and I slow to a stop, pulling over as best I can on this country road lined with deep ditches.

Just when I don't know whether I'm about to faint or throw up, the squad car gathers speed and passes me, lights still flashing.

He disappears over a hill, but I'm still stopped, my heart thumping wildly.

I throw my head back, look up through the open sun roof at the stars and say, "Thank you thank you thank you."

ONE WACKY PLANET

Okay, picture this: Where I live, the sun rises slowly through the trees behind my house and sets with a thud on the Blue Ridge Mountains beyond my front yard.

There's this disturbing dream that I have from time to time: I wake up, and it's morning. I look out my bathroom window and see the sun rising over the pond beside my house.

The sun is rising in the *north.*

My heart does a slow pirouette in my chest as I wonder: Is this the end of the world? And I think: Maybe I should report this to someone. The authorities. Yeah, that's it, to the authorities. Someone should do something about this.

I have a similar irrational response every December as the days grow disturbingly shorter. It's dark out, and I glance at my watch and see that it's only five o'clock in the afternoon.

My first reaction—fleeting but intense—is: What's going on? Maybe I should report this to someone. Of course, this is not a dream, and it takes only a nanosecond to remember that we're getting close to the winter solstice and this is supposed to happen.

I've been living on this planet for forty-five years. You'd think I'd have caught on by now.

THY NEIGHBORS' GOODS

Did you ever go on one of those Garden Week tours? I don't especially care about the gardens, but I love it when the tour includes someone's house.

A couple of years ago, our local tour included the house of one of my neighbors. I wasn't about to miss this. I run into these people all the time in the post office, but they've never invited me to their house.

On the day of the tour, I joined busloads of garden-lovers, trampling the grass and nodding politely as a guide told us about the English cottage garden. She said it's a place for ordered chaos.

Ordered chaos? I liked the sound of that.

Finally, we got to the good part—the house. The owners were nowhere in sight and guides were stationed strategically to steer people away from certain rooms and toward others.

This was a big, solid house with high ceilings. Original artwork covered the walls in the front hallway. Fragile-looking antique chairs flanked the front door.

Already, my own cluttered house seemed crummy compared to this.

My whole life seemed crummy compared to this.

We gathered in the living room where a guide told us the history of the house. I looked around the room and realized how wrong I had been about my neighbors. When I see them at the post office, they drive up in a dusty Jeep, wearing old jeans and T-shirts. Normal people, like me. Or so I thought.

I scanned the room, looking for a television, or a radio. Nothing. Not even a TV-sized cabinet where one could be hiding. This was not my kind of living room.

This was the kind of living room where the people have statues. And, yes, there were statues—a pair of skinny wrought-iron horses—perched on their own little mahogany table next to the fireplace.

I don't know about you, but you won't find any statues in *my* house. I have nothing against them, it's just that every month after we pay the mortgage, there's not much left over to put into the statue fund.

I do have an inflatable-doll version of *The Scream* on my mantel, and there's a trophy that I'd rather not discuss, but I don't think either of those qualify as statues.

Neatly displayed on their coffee table were several issues of *Smithsonian Magazine* and a stack of *Architectural Digests*. I happen to like both of those magazines, but I would have liked these people a whole lot better if there had also been, say, a current *TV Guide* or a *People* magazine.

I was not proud of myself for harboring these thoughts. After all, why should I think badly of these people just because they have more money and better taste than I do?

It was time to move on. The herd was shuffling toward the custom kitchen–a kitchen with an oven that cost more than my car.

I was about to pass through the doorway and leave the dining room, when I glanced up at their bookshelves. What I saw made me rethink everything I'd learned on this tour.

There, on the very top shelf, was a row of books, each one

with those tell-tale fat horizontal stripes stacked up the spine. *Reader's Digest Condensed Books.*

Hah!

How much do you want to bet that the TV was stashed away in one of those off-limits rooms? No wonder they were guarding those doors. They didn't want anybody to see their stacks of *People* magazines.

What else do you suppose they swept out of the way for Garden Week? Maybe a collection of barnyard-animal salt and pepper shakers. Or a clock in the shape of a beer bottle.

Back home, I looked around and decided that my place wasn't so bad, even though I have no gardens to speak of and my only antique is a 1950s-era chrome-and-vinyl dinette chair that belonged to my grandmother. I use it to stand on when I'm cleaning the cobwebs out of the corner of the ceiling.

I took a good look at my kitchen, and it made me smile to realize that all of our original artwork is home-grown and stuck to the refrigerator with magnets.

All things considered, I prefer the ordered chaos of my country cottage.

And all the novels on my shelves are full-length.

EARTHQUAKE?

EARTHQUAKE!

It was April 21st, the evening before Earth Day, when from five miles under the ground—under my house, as it turns out—there came a prolonged, thunderous roar. The earth growled for several seconds. The chair I was sitting on vibrated—the whole house vibrated. Was that thunder? Not quite. An explosion? Maybe.

And then the phone calls began. Did you hear that? Did you feel it? What was it?

My son, Waldo, began his own succession of phone calls: to the police (who were flooded with calls), to radio stations, the newspaper. The radio stations and newspaper seemed to think my son was a lunatic. Explosion? Earthquake? They knew nothing and appeared not to have the slightest twinge of curiosity.

When the TV's eight-o'clock news update made no mention of the possible quake, Waldo called the station. Get this: The TV people had heard about the great rumble—and had been ready to jump into the van with their ActionCam—when it occurred to them that there was nothing to photograph, so they decided not to pursue the story.

Waldo said, "Look, say something about it. Everyone thinks they're crazy, that they imagined the whole thing."

On the 11 o'clock news, here's what they said: If you heard and felt a big boom at 7:28 this evening, you're not losing your mind. According to the police, a pair of jets was seen in the area. It was a sonic boom.

At this point, my son and I were shouting at the television. "No way! It wasn't a boom—it was a rumble. It wasn't jets. They just made that up. Somebody just made that up and the TV station ran with it. How hard could it be to research this? There must be a Web site for the U.S. Geological Survey. They would know instantly."

Next morning, the newspaper parroted the same lame explanation. Whatever happened to research? If that wasn't an earthquake, I'll eat that newspaper.

Nearly twenty-four hours after the mysterious rumble, a TV reporter who finally checked the geology Web site told us that, yes indeedy, it was an earthquake. 2.5 on the Richter scale, and it was centered smack in the middle of our little hamlet.

Well, the biggest event around here is the tiny Fourth of July parade that has more people marching in it than watching it.

So, the quake may have been a magnitude 2.5—laughable by California standards. But, around here, this *experience* was a magnitude 8.5. Possibly a 10.

As we continued to rant about the clueless media, I began to wonder why I cared so much. Why did it matter to me whether or not this earthquake made the news?

Apparently, I want them to tell me what I already know.

If something I went through is reported in the news, then it must be important. Therefore, I am important.

Pitiful, isn't it? Like a grown-up child still looking to Mommy and Daddy to say, "Yes, dear, that really was a big, scary dog that barked at you! Yes, indeed."

Today, as I stood on my porch and looked above the treetops at the south slope of Buck Mountain, ground zero for the Great Virginia Earthquake, I wondered: If a tree falls in the forest, and the TV ActionCam isn't there to record the event, did it really happen?

PONDSCUM

It's August twelfth, two days before my son's wedding. Two days before my entire Yankee family—including my mother—will visit my home for the first time. I've bragged about my rural Virginia house, how it overlooks a deep, half-acre pond that mirrors the trees and sky.

Already, I've scrubbed every inch of my house, even painted the front porch. Now, do I want them to see how I *really* live? Nuh-uh. I want them to see perfection. To see the little sister who's done good.

As I stand back to behold my flawless domain, I look over at the pond. Ah, yes. The pond. The reflective pond that is now thickly carpeted with a kind of scum called pond meal. It's a flat, luminous-green mat, like a putting green.

Disgusting.

Months ago, with this project in mind, I bought an entire bolt of wedding-veil netting. Here's what I planned: On a windy day, when the scum has blown over to one small section of the pond, we could stretch the netting across one end of the pond and scoop all that gunk up and out of the water. How hard could this be?

Today, the groom's available to help. However, there's not a breath of wind. Maybe I should just forget about this. Accept the pond for what it is.

Then, I imagine my mother inspecting the pond on Saturday, sadly shaking her head, saying, "Too bad about that swamp over there. . . . "

I see no choice but to gather up every extension cord in the house, stringing them together so I can place our two oscillating fans next to the water: Instant wind! I'm a genius. We wait several minutes, but the scum doesn't budge. Hm. I readjust one of the fans. It plunges head first into the water. Well, forget that. I pull the plugs.

Jackson takes one end of the netting and ties it to our canoe. I balance on the steep bank and unroll the bolt. Jack tries a tricky maneuver . . . and flips the canoe over.

Just as I'm imagining my distraught phone call to his fiancée, Jack pops up out of the water, laughing, his face and glasses covered in green slime.

After some struggling, we're pulling the netting and gathering up an impressive and heavy load of scum. All right! But wait, the water behind the netting is still that nasty green.

Turns out that our particular variety of pond scum is so fine that most of it just slips right through the net.

We haul our catch of scum and assorted wildlife to the edge of the pond. It stinks. It's slimy. It has made absolutely no difference in the pond. Jack insists that we comb through our harvest to rescue the little animals. I leave that to him. I've had it.

Well, Saturday came and went. Great reunion, wonderful wedding, huge success all around.

My mother called today. "Gee," she said, "too bad about that swamp . . . right next to your house and all. . . . "

A SNOOTFUL OF SALT AIR

I sit here, a spoiled child in paradise, rocking on my shady porch overlooking the foothills of the Blue Ridge Mountains in Virginia. An iridescent hummingbird hovers at the feeder, then wraps his little toes around the perch for a few seconds, resting his busy wings.

This is heaven. So, how could I wish to be someplace else? And yet, on this hot summer afternoon, I close my eyes and try to summon the sights, sounds, and smells of the ocean.

And not just any ocean. Not just any beach. I'm very particular about my daydreams.

I have gone to the seashore in Hawaii, Jamaica, Florida, and South Carolina and come away disappointed. Why? Because in none of those places could I smell the ocean.

Imagine going to a wonderful Italian restaurant when you have a bad cold, a stuffed-up nose. The food looks good, but without a snootful of air laced with garlicky tomato sauce and fresh, yeasty bread, who cares?

Like the ocean that has no salt smell, better you should stay home and look at pictures of food–or of the ocean–in a magazine. Less fat and less disappointment.

In the ocean setting that I conjure up in my mountain-bound home, the air is heavy with a bracing saltiness and carries that decaying smell of low tide that reminds you how temporary it all is.

This is the intoxicating atmosphere of Cape Ann, Massachusetts.

I grew up in a town about an hour west of there and, with my family, made frequent pilgrimages to Gloucester, on Cape Ann, every summer.

To a kid with a poor sense of time and direction, there was nothing—nothing—that could beat the thrill of riding past an ordinary flat landscape of stores, churches, and houses, and without warning, discovering that relentlessly flat blue horizon—a surreal backdrop—behind ordinary houses. Stunning, every time.

And soon, a gust of cooler, salty air blows in through the car and there I am, filling my lungs to bursting with this salt-sweet air—as if I could save some for later—and I'm limp against the back seat, thinking: Yes! Oh, yes! I made it. I'm back.

Climbing up the hot, sandy path, past flat pink wild roses, I hear it: The rhythmic crash and sizzle, then ominous silence of incoming waves.

We spread out our blanket (actually a white chenille bedspread) and I race toward the water.

At more southerly beaches, a person can go sashaying right on into the water. It's that warm. But where is the challenge in that?

I sprint in up to my ankles, stay for a second or two—until my ankles ache—then sprint out again. I repeat this cycle a dozen times, going a little deeper each time, until my whole body aches, then goes happily numb.

The ocean at Gloucester is typically Yankee: assertive, in-your-face, challenging.

And I miss it.

I have this fantasy: That the publishing world will briefly turn away from producing books by basketball players, murderers, and disgraced politicians and pay a small fortune for *my* novels. Then, I will keep my Blue Ridge country cottage with its mountain view and hummingbirds, and I'll buy me a summer house on Cape Ann.

Nothing fancy, just an ordinary house—but with that surreal backdrop of relentlessly flat blue ocean. And when the wind is right, a snootful of salty air.

It could happen.

IN DEFENSE OF POSSUMS

Fox Haven, Fox Chase, Fox Run, Cross Fox. You've seen these signs, haven't you? Why do all these ritzy estates have "fox" in their names? Like the fox is some kind of aristocratic animal. What's up with *that*? Can't you just picture a fox wearing Italian loafers and a Rolex watch, his manicured little paws on the steering wheel of a Range Rover, looking smug?

Let's blame the English for this. Or the rich, idle English. They started the tradition of galloping through the countryside, scaring the bejeebers out of foxes.

A more appropriate animal to honor in this way would be the possum.

After all, possums provided sustenance for early settlers. And they were cooperative prey—you didn't need any horses to catch one, that's for sure.

The possum is more of a democratic, all-American animal. I picture a possum behind the wheel of an old pickup truck, some well-earned dirt under his claws. And of course, the kids are always along for the ride.

So, you think the owners of these estates would go for it? Possum Haven, Possum Chase, Possum Run, Cross Possum.

Just this morning I passed a sign at the end of a long driveway. The sign said, "Dogpatch."

I don't know who lives there, but I'm pretty sure I'd like those people.

OUT OF ORDER

My phone is out of order—for the third time in two months.

No, its not my actual telephone, it's the wires between me and civilization. These lines, I'm told, need to be replaced. But that would cost the phone company a whole lot of money, so instead, they continue to patch them up somehow. I think what they use is that white paste we had in first grade, the kind of paste that some kids eat.

When the phone is dead, I go into a panic. What if? I imagine someone at my daughter's school dialing my number, wanting desperately to tell me to meet them at the emergency room. Instead, all they hear is my phone ringing and ringing and ringing. They must think I'm a horribly irresponsible mother, that I've unplugged the answering machine, or I'm having a long, gossipy conversation with a girlfriend, ignoring all the call-waiting beeps.

In the olden days, if a line was temporarily out of service, you'd get a recorded message from an operator telling you so. No more. To have such a helpful, informative message put on my line is impossible, says my chipper repair service representative.

I don't believe for one second that this is impossible. The phone company has technology up the wazoo, and they can't put an out-of-order message on my line? Give me a break.

As the day wears on, I imagine every important phone call that I've ever wanted to receive sabotaged by the phone company.

I'm sure that a publisher—Doubleday, no doubt—is frantically trying to get through to me. They want *both* my novels and I must tell them yes or no today, or forget about it, they'll publish someone else's stories.

Or that some old boyfriend who broke my heart years ago has chosen today—*today*—to look me up and give me a call. Right now, I'm probably missing a golden opportunity to say, "Drop dead. I'm married." and hang up on him.

I need to calm down. I'm trying. Give me a second.

The other day, on Oprah, there was this woman who has written a book about living a spiritual life. (Apparently, this woman's call from Doubleday went through . . .). She said that when these things happen, things like out-of-order phones, that we are being given a gift, a lesson, and we should close our eyes, breathe deeply and ask ourselves, "What am I supposed to learn from this?"

Okay, I'm going to do that right now. . . . I'm taking a deep breath . . .

What am I supposed to learn from this? I hope the answer is something wise and profound. . . . Nothing yet. Oh, wait. I'm getting something: The lesson I'm supposed to be learning is . . .

. . . to get a voice mailbox.

A voice mailbox? That's my cosmic message? Hold on, the phone company can't put an out-of-order message on my phone line, but they can plant a commercial message like that in my brain?

I *told* you they had technology up the wazoo!

I'M NOT CRAZY

It was my first winter in Virginia. There was a blizzard—a humdinger of a blizzard—that left me as helpless and vulnerable as an infant.

The power was out for days and I discovered what life without electricity—and worse, life without water—can be like.

We wandered around in our frigid house in near-darkness, my husband and I and our three children, and I felt very, very stupid. Every time I walked past a lamp or a machine or a faucet I thought: How has it come to this?

My grandmother would have known what to do. She was born into a manually-operated world. I was born into a push-button world.

In the space of two generations, we have become so dependent on technology, which is to say, on other people, that we are as helpless as babies when the power's cut off. And, when you think about it, power is an alarmingly accurate word for electricity.

I have nothing against electricity; it's my total dependence on it that drives me crazy.

In other places I've lived, power lines are underground, and the electrical supply is reliable. In Virginia, power lines are strung up in the air, and these threads that connect us to our electrical supply are frequently snapped by ice and wind, falling trees and wayward vehicles. Not only are our homes affected, but the gas pumps we need—in order to drive someplace where there *is* electricity—won't operate without it.

And, have you ever been in a store when the power goes off? I have pleaded with clerks to accept my money so I can take what I need and be on my way. But, no, the cash registers are electric, and the clerks are completely helpless without a machine to figure out the change for them.

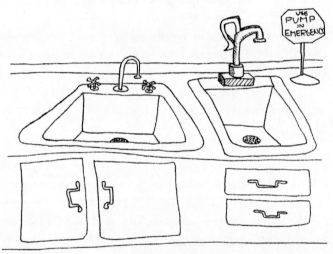

I'm not crazy.

The worst part about being without electricity is that we can't get water from our well. The pump, of course, is electric. You can't flush a toilet or wash up or make a cup of coffee. I hate this.

And so, I have taken up a new hobby: emergency preparedness. My friends think I'm crazy. They think I'm becoming obsessed with this. But, should we lose electricity this winter, *I'll* be the one with a good supply of firewood to fuel my brand-new wood stove.

The stove keeps us warm and I can cook on top of it, if I have to. I have a few boxes filled with canned food, canned juices, and bottled water. I have a couple of lanterns, several flashlights, and lots of batteries.

But my favorite emergency-preparedness toy is a windup radio. You turn the crank about 60 times and the radio runs for nearly an hour. AM, FM, and shortwave. It's not exactly lifesaving, but it could save my sanity when we're wondering how wide-spread the outage is and when the power is expected to come back on.

One area I'm still deficient in is water. Bottled water helps, but for a prolonged power outage, it's impossible to store up all the water you'll need in gallon jugs.

I'd feel much better if there were some kind of manual override for my water pump. I know, a generator would help, but I'm thinking about long-term power interruptions, because, when you run out of gasoline for the generator, you're done for.

I called the people who put in our well to ask for advice, and the woman who answered the phone thought I was a lunatic for wanting a manually-operated water pump. I asked her to pass my message on to the owner, but he never called back.

Look, I just want to be able to take care of my family during an emergency. Is that so crazy? I think that this is the very heart and soul of sanity: taking responsibility, planning ahead.

I don't want to feel powerless when the power goes off, that's all.

I'm not crazy.

GETAWAY

I got a call from a friend the other day. He lives in Massachusetts and it was snowing there when he called, so I was feeling pretty smug about living here in balmy Virginia.

After a few comments about problems with work and kids, I said, "So, what have you been up to these days?" His voice brightened as he said, "I went to the Caribbean. For a week." This man is going through a divorce, so the next question had to be asked. "Alone?" I said. With a lilt in his voice that was close to music, he said, "No. I went with Genevieve." Genevieve is the name of his post-separation girlfriend.

My first thought was: Oh, man. Other people are single and they're flying off to warm beaches with new lovers and here I am married forever and the most exotic trip I've taken lately is buying my groceries at Foods of All Nations.

I didn't ask for a single detail of his trip. I wouldn't give him the satisfaction. After I hung up, my visions of canoodling on beaches at sunset and sipping piña coladas from the same pineapple with two straws were slowly invaded by remembrances of travel. Real travel, not fantasies or rosy, altered memories of travel.

In my experience, travel, particularly when it involves a foreign country, includes endless expanses of boredom while waiting and waiting at airports, and then there are those airplane seats that fit like a strait jacket, and I always seem to end up sweating out connecting flights.

I find that even with the best of companions, one of us is becoming a little snippy by the time we're waiting around for the van that might show up and take us to our hotel.

And the flights aren't so great, either. During takeoffs and landings, I'm in the habit of praying out loud. My seatmates sometimes find this unnerving.

The first few minutes of being in a hotel are fun, what with jumping on the bed and discovering the bathrobes and hairdryer. But then there's the time between unpacking and dinner, when he's in the bathroom, or downstairs complaining about something, and I get this pang of loneliness. Knowing that I don't belong in this strange room and where do I belong, anyway? What am I doing here?

And then, in the course of having this fabulous fun-in-the-sun week together, there are all those small negotiations that go into any decent relationship.

"Let's stay on the beach."

"I'm sick of the beach. Let's go shopping."

Pretty soon, someone is sulking and ruining something for the other person. And so it goes.

And the handholding on the flight down turns into sitting, lost in your own thoughts on the way home.

And when we get home, the testiness, the loneliness, the small squabbles, the annoyances that arise from sharing a bathroom, the memories of all this fade faster than our suntans.

But it sounds good, doesn't it? A week in the Caribbean.

Hm . . . I wonder how much that would cost?

TURN OFF THOSE DAMNED FLOODLIGHTS

My neighbors are driving me crazy.

Let me explain. I live way out in the boondocks of Virginia. Or, at least, I used to. I built the first house in this untouched paradise, and for a few years, all I saw from my house was mountains and woods and pond.

Except at night.

At night, I saw a black velvet sky hung thick with fat stars. I saw the nebula in Orion's sword, all seven sisters of the Pleiades, and the broad, jagged path of the Milky Way.

Even while lying in bed at night, I could look across the room at my window and see a tall rectangle of stars.

I have routinely seen the Big Dipper reflected in the glassy surface of the pond.

So, imagine how I felt a few years ago, when I rushed through dinner in order to stand on my front porch and have a look at the Hale-Bopp comet.

This paradise of mine has become a sprawling

neighborhood, with three houses visible through the trees. During daylight hours, they all but disappear. Nighttime is another story.

My neighbors, like me, have escaped to this rural area from suburbia. Unlike me, my neighbors are afraid of the dark. They illuminate their houses on all sides with blinding floodlights.

Out here in the boondocks, far from the road, your neighbors are too far away to see someone skulking around your house. If anything, the floodlights make a burglar's work easier, revealing the window you've left open or the ladder at the back of the house.

So, here I am, settling onto the bottom step of my front porch, when I look up and, squinting into the glare, I count five floodlights blazing at me from these three houses.

Unwilling to give up, I cover my eyes with my hands for a few seconds, allowing my pupils to dilate, and then raise my forearm to eye level, trying to block the lights from all three houses.

I am moderately successful. I think I see the comet. It looks like a smeared star with a suggestion of a tail.

My heart heavy with exasperation and a kind of grief, I give up and go back in the house. Big deal. A blurry star. My sky-struck days are over.

But wait. A few days later, I pull into my driveway in the early evening. I'm heading for the house, struggling with an overloaded bag of groceries, when I look up, and I'm overtaken by the rich blackness of the evening—and by the heavy spattering of silver stars. A miracle has happened: My neighbors' houses are dark, invisible.

And high above the treetops I see it—this imposing, show-off star, a feathery white peacock trailing an extravagant tail that grows longer and longer as I stand there in the chill stillness, my arms wrapped around the bag of groceries.

And I am profoundly grateful to witness this, grateful to

be alive and in this place at this moment.

I should probably tell my neighbors how much their lights bother me, or better yet, how much they're missing.

But I would rather have them hear it on the radio than tell them face to face.

And so, the next time I make a wish on the first star of the evening, I know what I'll wish for.

More stars.

FUN WITH CHICKEN BONES

Oh, that seductive smell: The palpable, come-hither aroma of chicken, roasting. I'm at the supermarket to buy a bottle of vitamins, but the invisible olfactory river of roasting chicken sweeps me up and carries me to the back corner of the store. Mmm, mmm . . . Gotta get me some of that.

Suddenly, I'm so hungry that I find myself tossing things into my basket on the way to the chicken department. A bag of Oreos, a carton of Cherry Garcia, Cheez Doodles. At last, I bag a rotisserie chicken and head home.

After our no-fuss dinner of chicken and Cheez Doodles, Harry and I are cleaning up the kitchen.

He points to the chicken carcass and says, "You got any plans for that?"

I'm hoping he'll volunteer to boil up some chicken broth. "Knock yourself out," I say, reaching for the stock pot.

"Oh, no," he says, sticking the carcass into the fridge, "Tomorrow, I'm gonna use it on those pawpaw trees out front."

Now, I'm not sure where my husband's picking up his gardening tips these days, but get this: He wants to dismantle the carcass, tie strings to the bones, and hang them from the branches of our two little pawpaw trees.

The thing is, these trees are right out by the mailbox, where everyone going past can see them. What would you think, if you saw a neighbor's tree festooned with chicken bones? I'd think there was some kind of voodoo thing going on in that household, that's what I'd think.

But wait, Harry has an explanation:

This is a tree that can't get a date—because it's very fussy. Normally, the only creature that will arouse the pollen in the pawpaw is the Zebra Swallowtail. And unless you have a big pawpaw patch with lots of trees, this butterfly will sneer at your inadequate display and keep going.

So, if you ever want to sample the elusive fruit of the pawpaw tree, first, you have to act as a kind of dating service for it. The Zebra Swallowtail butterfly is the Tom Cruise of pollinators for the pawpaw, so, forget that. The next likely candidate is a way distant second best. It's the fly. Yes, what you chase after with a rolled-up newspaper, that's what the pawpaw needs for pollination.

But, are flies attracted to pawpaws? Heck, no. You have to entice them. Enter Harry and his chicken-carcass decorations.

I must admit that now that I know how desperate the poor thing is for pollination, I don't care if people think I have a screw loose.

As I'm tying a leg bone, with meat hanging off it, to a pawpaw branch, I'm imagining a fly, minding his own business, passing through the neighborhood—when he picks up the scent of chicken carcass.

"Mmm, mmm," he says. "Gotta get me some of that." Then, on the way to the chicken department, he can't help but pick up some pollen on his feet—and then we're in business.

Much like wandering through the grocery store: It's what happens on the *way* to the chicken that makes all the difference.

PART FOUR

I'M JUST SAYING . . .

I CAN STILL ZIP IT UP, I SWEAR

This happens every year. The weather turns warm, and I start to panic. I step on the scale more often, and start using weights when I exercise.

Now, I couldn't care less about bathing suits. I don't have a pool and I live far away from any beach.

This is the time of year when Harry and I celebrate our wedding anniversary.

I think of marriage as a contract, and a big part of the deal is appearance. Yeah, yeah, you love each other's heart and soul, but I bet there are lots of people with beautiful souls who you'd never even consider *dating*, let alone *marrying*.

Sure, you marry someone for the heart and soul stuff, but P.S., you *are* physically attracted to each other, right?

And so, I think that any major changes in a spouse's appearance are potential deal-breakers.

Lots of things are beyond our control, like hair loss,

wrinkles, illness, and injuries. We *can*, however, control how much we eat, and how fit we are.

With that in mind, my template for holding the line is my wedding dress.

Every anniversary, I drag out my polyester gown trimmed with cotton lace, and do my best to zip it up. I figure if I can manage to get the zipper closed, then I'm upholding my end of the contract.

One year, following a pregnancy, I was worried that I wouldn't make it. But I did it; I zipped it up. Okay, I needed help, and it involved some sweating and groaning, but I did it.

I should mention that my husband plays no part in this. He never has anything but compliments and I think he finds it somewhat bewildering to be married to me.

Anyway, last year I got it zipped but the short, lacey sleeves were awfully tight. I panicked, afraid I was going to get stuck inside those sleeves. Now, *that* would be embarrassing, having to be cut out of my wedding dress . . .

And this evening, I'll try it on once again, along with the veil and the white shoes—satin pumps that are now a full size too small.

My kids, before they escaped out into the world, would pray that Mummy would not choose a moment when their friends were visiting to sweep down the stairs, looking like a cross between Miss Havisham and a pair of white, polyester sausages.

Tonight, when Harry comes home from work, I'll put on our CD of *La Bohème*. I'll go right to the part that was played at our wedding.

Then, I'll go up into the attic and unhook the ghost that hangs from the rafter all year long, waiting for this moment to flow and swirl and dance one more time.

I'll descend the stairs, hoping that what he sees isn't a

middle–aged fool jammed into her wedding clothes, but a reminder of the person he chose all those years ago.

We'll dance for a bit to Puccini, reminisce awhile . . .

And then I hope to God I can take the thing off.

THE STARS AND
STRIPES ... FOREVER

I was rooting around in my underwear drawer this morning when I came across an American flag. Actually, it's a scarf someone gave me last Fourth of July, but it *is* an American flag. Stars, stripes, the works.

As it happened, the flag wasn't what I was looking for, so I dumped the drawer out on my bed. Buried among the socks and unmentionables I found a couple of other icons from my past: a broken rosary, and the scapular given to me by Sister Mary Margaret after I made my First Communion.

I found the item I was looking for, and as I was stuffing everything back into the drawer, I vowed to clean it out one of these days. But I know I'll never throw away the rosary or the scapular.

After all, they've been blessed. And besides, as soon as I hung that scapular around my neck, Sister Mary Margaret warned me—warned the whole class—never to take that scapular off. Never. She told us we should keep it on whether we were in the shower, or at the beach. No matter what.

The worst thing that could happen to us, she said, was if we were to die, and not be wearing that scapular. Then, we would go straight to Hell.

Of course, the Catholic Church has changed a lot in the ensuing forty years. And, if the truth be told, I never did believe Sister Mary Margaret. As soon as I got home that day, I took off the scapular. But I didn't dare to throw it away.

Same deal with the palm leaves that were handed out at Mass every year on Palm Sunday. The priest blessed them, we took them home—and then what? I think every picture in our house was garnished with a desiccated palm frond stuck between the frame and the wall.

But what about the American-flag scarf? To tell you the truth, it wouldn't bother me to throw that away. I looked pretty silly in it anyway, and it just doesn't have the kind of religious magic that I attribute to my old Catholic artifacts.

I'm a little worried about the actual disposal of it, though. Some of our elected friends in Washington are trying to amend the Constitution so they can pass laws that would make it a crime to desecrate the American flag. When I heard this on the news, I looked up "desecrate." Here's what my dictionary says: "to divert from a sacred to a common usage."

Hm. Sacred?

If that amendment passes, and I toss my little flag into the trash, or into an incinerator, I don't suppose anyone would come after me.

Because they wouldn't know.

However, if I handled the flag in a way that called attention to the fact that I was, say, ripping it up or burning it, then I'd be in trouble. That would be a kind of political statement. Political speech, you might say. Then, they could toss me into prison.

This makes Sister Mary Margaret's threat of an eternity in Hell seem tame by comparison. Because, lucky for me, no one gave *her* the executive power to carry out that particular punishment.

QUACK

I'm zooming down the highway, happily listening to the news, when a wave of nausea overtakes me. Is it something I ate? I don't think so.

No, the source of my nausea is something I just heard on the radio. An interview with a political candidate. And, no, it's not the candidate himself who makes me ill, it's what he just said. It's two words. Brace yourself, I'm about to utter them.

Family values.

Ooof.

Family Values. Am I the only one who gags at hearing those words? Candidates are hitting me over the head with family, family, family. I suppose it's intended to give me a warm, fuzzy feeling and want to vote for them so I can be included in this family thing.

There are people who have run for office—and won—who managed to say absolutely nothing about any issue, all the while yammering incessantly about families. "My opponent spent the last term in office undermining family values. A vote for Joe Schmoe is a vote for the American family."

Oh, bite me!

Tell me, Mr. Schmoe, how does this distinguish you from anyone else who's running? Who is *not* part of a family? Who are you trying to exclude, here, huh? . . . orphans? It's like saying, "A vote for Joe Schmoe is a vote for human beings!" Well, duh, who else would you be representing? Martians? Rocks?

I truly believe that, if the spin doctors and advertising people told these candidates that talking about fuzzy ducks would win them votes, they'd say, "A vote for Joe Schmoe is a vote for fuzzy ducks! Look at my opponent's voting record. He has done everything possible to undermine fuzzy ducks."

I'd like to witness a political race where the word *family* was verboten. What would they talk about then? Oh my God . . . they'd have to talk about issues. They'd have to talk about which laws they plan to create and, better yet, which laws they plan to get rid of.

Imagine that!

Picture a candidate getting up and saying, "You know, those sodomy laws are an invasion of privacy, I'll get rid of them if you elect me." Or, how about this one, "Let's rethink this whole policy of sending people to jail for using drugs. Maybe there's some other way we can help them."

Hah, that ain't gonna happen.

But think of the controversy! Imagine the lively debates! Now, that would be an election that everyone, whether pro or con, would find engaging. And a lot more people would vote.

Hey, I have an idea. Maybe we can get them to lay off this family values thing. What they need is feedback. Whenever a candidate starts braying about families, wouldn't it be great if someone in the crowd would start quacking like a duck? If only one person quacks, people will just think he's nuts, but if two people quack, we may be onto something. And can you imagine fifty people—I said fifty people—standing up and quacking like ducks. Pretty soon, the whole crowd will be quacking. And friends, when that happens, we'll have ourselves a movement.

Which is kind of like a family, only louder.

. . . but if two people quack, we may be onto something . . .

LICENSE TO WORRY

My daughter just got her learner's permit, so now I have something new to worry about. Not that I'm a worrier, really. My mother's a worrier. But I'm not like my mother.

Of course, I worry about my kids. Who doesn't worry about their kids? I worry they'll turn out all wrong, and it'll be all my fault—and to tell you the truth, I'm also worried that I left the iron on this morning, and my house will be reduced to a smoldering heap and I'll have no place to go and I'll end up living out on the street like those poor wretched souls I see wandering around in the city, pushing shopping carts full of everything they own and I worry that I haven't donated enough to the Salvation Army or the food pantry—which is very bad karma for me getting food and shelter once *I'm* out on the street—plus, I worry about the ozone layer and wonder whether we'll all end up crusted over with skin cancers and what's the deal anyway with frogs disappearing all over the planet—what's next, *us?* And I'm worried about Y2K—will all the computers shut down and leave us in the dark? And when will the lights come back on and why am *I* the only one who's worried about this? And I worry about the tightness in my chest that I'm feeling right now. I can't tell if the tightness is *above* the sternum or *below* the sternum and that's important because *below* the sternum means you're having a heart attack and my father had his first heart attack at thirty-nine and here I am forty-six . . . and if I should drop dead RIGHT NOW who will take care of the people I love? Who will my friends turn to for advice? Who will comfort my bereaved husband? Who will mother my children? Somebody else, that's who. I worry that no one really needs me and wouldn't miss me anyway. I could be abducted by aliens and no one would notice and, by the way, those people who say they were abducted by aliens— what if they're NOT crazy? And I worry that right this minute, someone I love is hurt or in trouble and I'm not there to help and I'll feel guilty about it for the rest of my life, as well I should.

What was I thinking, letting my daughter get her learner's permit? She'll get her license and she'll be hurt or in trouble and I'll be nowhere in sight. What kind of mother am I?

CRASH TEST

Don't ever give me a ride in your car. You will regret it. When I sit in a moving car with no steering wheel in my hands and no brake under my foot, I feel like I'm in a runaway vehicle. I wince and gasp and mutter things like, "Sweet mother of God . . . " At every approach to an intersection, I squeeze my eyes shut and wait for the impact.

It is with this in mind that I will tell you about my field trip to Ruckersville, Virginia. Ruckersville is the home of the Insurance Institute for Highway Safety. The home and playground of crash-test dummies. I went there for the express purpose of watching a car crash.

As I walk from my car to the building, I am hoping that this experience will be a kind of immersion therapy for me. That it will fix me. Make me brave.

I join the tour, and we are led to the green room, where crash-test dummies sit patiently, lined up against a wall, calmly awaiting their moment in the spotlight.

I envy the composure of the dummies. They have been pinned between steering columns and seat backs, rocketed through windshields. They have experienced every one of my waking nightmares. And yet they sit there, calm, their identical faces both peaceful and alert.

We are led to a hall the size of an airplane hangar, and climb up onto a catwalk that straddles a long track. The track leads to a huge block of cement with a smaller block of metal attached to it. Soon, a Kia Sportage—a Korean sports utility vehicle—will smack into this block.

Our guide explains to us the mechanics of a crash like this. Tells us which parts of the vehicle should remain rigid and which parts should collapse like a beer can under your foot.

There's a countdown, and the lights dim. Around the intended impact area, banks of intensely bright lights switch on. The effect is eerie, other-worldly. It looks like the site of a top-secret missile launch.

Three . . . two . . . one . . . zero. At the far end of the track, a garage door slides open. The Kia appears—it's cherry red. In eight seconds it has accelerated to nearly forty miles per hour as it passes right under the catwalk I'm standing on.

This is so cool!

And then—BAM—it hits the block. The sound it makes is not a crash. It's a tremendous, percussive POP that smacks me in the chest. Wow. And nobody got hurt.

We descend to the crash site, and inspect the damage. The front end is history, but the passenger compartment looks surprisingly good. And the dummy isn't complaining.

Suddenly, I'm an expert who knows what to look for in the aftermath of a crash. Sizing up the wreckage, sizing up the dummy.

So this is therapeutic, after all. Now that I understand the mechanics of a crash, have seen how effectively an airbag and seatbelt work, I will be a brave passenger.

On the way out, we're given a sheaf of handouts to take home with us.

That evening, the brochures and charts are spread out

in front of me. Most riveting is one called "Driver Death Rates." You look up your vehicle and find out how likely you are to die in your car. It is not a pretty picture.

My new-found confidence leaks out of me like antifreeze from a bad radiator. I look up my own car and say, "Ah, jeez . . . " I look up my husband's car and mutter, "Sweet mother of God . . . "

I was right, all along. Automobiles are death traps. If I have be in a car, I want a steering wheel in my hands, and a brake pedal under my foot.

Is that so much to ask?

HEART—BEAT!

I am drifting through sleep, my mind engaged in one of those stupid, nonsensical dreams that are a waste of good dream time, when I wake up, and I just know that I have to get up and move around, or I will die. I know something is wrong with my heart. I think it has stopped beating.

I leap out of bed and pace furiously for a few seconds, in a desperate attempt to seize control of my body, to force this strange feeling—this feeling that I'm suddenly dying—to pass. It doesn't. And I'm shouting, "Oh! Oh! Oh my God! It's not working, it's not going away!"

Now, my husband's awake. He has flipped the light on and he's kneeling on the edge of the mattress, looking panicked and helpless. I'm standing there in the long white nightgown my mother gave me for Christmas. And I'm thinking: How appropriate, I'm already dressed in my ghost costume.

I feel myself slipping away, sinking, like Leonardo DiCaprio slipping off the driftwood from the Titanic, unable to hold onto this world any longer. I'm dying, and I don't know what I'm supposed to grab onto. I'm feeling nothing where my heart should be. A horrifying void is spreading out, overtaking my chest.

When the void spreads upward to my head, I lean forward into my husband's arms and I say, "In case I don't make it: I love you." And I'm sinking, and at the same time I'm feeling buoyant, less dense, but still slipping away. I'm dying.

With a powerful lurch, my heart takes control, and it thumps and thumps and thumps, each thump a desperate apology for having abandoned me like that, for letting me float off toward a place where heartbeats don't matter.

I lie back in bed as my heart's now-diligent pumping grows softer and more regular. Slowly, my heart chants: I'm sorry, I'm sorry, I'm sorry. And I rest my right hand over my heart, as if to soothe it, and we promise, my heart and I, to take care of one another from now on.

Yes, yes, yes, I *will* call the doctor in the morning, first thing. I promise, yes.

And this interior, rhythmic massage sends me drifting along the safe, happy surface of consciousness, where I fall into one of those wonderful, nonsensical dreams, as my husband's face hovers over mine: vigilant, grateful, worried.

WHAT WERE THEY THINKING?

When my son was three years old, he went tearing down the aisle of a store and slammed into a man who was minding his own business. A man who, it turned out, had a wooden leg. Jack knocked the prosthesis out from under this man, who then fell flat on the floor.

If remorse could kill, I would have dropped dead at that moment.

I tried to help, but the man, furious, waved us away. I hissed to my son, "Say you're sorry!" My three-year-old raised his chin defiantly and said, "No! It was an accident. I didn't mean it."

I found my son's behavior confusing, incomprehensible. What was he thinking? How could I be related to this monster? And so, even though I had said it dozens of times during this endless minute since my son smacked into him, I turned to the man and said, "I am so sorry."

I couldn't change the world-view of a three-year-old, but

I could set an example; show my son that, in the adult world, we express regret and compassion whether the events are caused by us or by someone else—whether intentional or accidental.

A while back, President Clinton contemplated apologizing to African-Americans on behalf of the government of the United States.

I know just how he feels. When I think of the way our forefathers behaved, I find it confusing, incomprehensible. What were they thinking? Putting chains on people and tossing them into the holds of ships like so much lumber. Buying and selling human beings and calling themselves Christians. What was that all about?

And it wasn't so long ago. The repercussions are still causing pain. And so, how hard could it be, for those of us whose families have not felt the pain of enslavement, to say:

We are sorry. We are all so very sorry.

WATCH OUT

When I was a kid, my sister, Patty, and I were forbidden to play on the railroad tracks, because, as everyone knows, railroad tracks are very dangerous.

Whenever we'd play over there, on the railroad tracks, we'd crouch down and lay one ear on the metal rail.

If a train was coming, but was too far away to be seen or heard, the track would produce a subtle vibration that was almost a sound. The cool metal whispered against my ear.

When I felt that whisper, I felt like I was in on some important secret. A train was coming, and only Patty and I knew it. Sometimes, though, we'd feel the track whisper, but no train appeared. Maybe it switched off to another track, I really don't know. In any case, once we felt that sound, it seemed like a real good idea to get away from those tracks.

I never regretted the decision to run, whether a train showed up or not.

I haven't laid an ear on a railroad track in decades, but there have been times when I've had that same whisper-in-the-rail feeling. There's something in the distance that's not a rumble, not close enough to be heard, just a tiny, distinct, vibration. And it can be chilling. Especially when no one else hears it or feels it.

The faint, but strange, little sound coming from my car's engine.

The barely perceptible tinge of green on dark storm clouds.

The tiny sound upstairs when I thought I had come home to an empty house.

When I ignore these signs, I often regret it.

For months now, there's been a lot of talk about the so-called Y2K problem: how all the computers are supposed to crash at midnight on December 31, 1999. For a long time, I turned a deaf ear to all that technical stuff.

I know nothing about computers, and I figured that *they* would take care of it. They always do, don't they? The computer whizzes, the government—somebody.

A couple of weeks ago, I came across a report about this Y2K thing in the newspaper. Merrill Lynch and a computer services firm sized up different industries to see if they're ready for 2000. *Will* these businesses be able to fix their computers before they all shut down? Merrill Lynch looked at industries such as financial services, health care, and electric utilities. Guess which one was found to be the least prepared? Merrill Lynch gave a thumbs down to electric utilities. They're not ready and they're not saying how they intend to *get* ready.

Well, now. Who cares if banking, health care, and everyone else is ready to deal with the problem if the power companies aren't? Try to run a bank or a hospital without power. Try to run your business, or pump gas, or take care of your family without it.

And how long might we be without electricity? Beats me. How long will it take them to fix all the lines of computer code and to find and replace all those embedded computer chips that will stop working at midnight?

Maybe I'm getting myself all worked up about a train that will never come down this track. Still, I feel that slight vibration in the rail. That little whisper.

SHOPPING AT THE DUMP

Are you looking for that last-minute gift for someone special? Well, I have a shopping tip for you that you will not hear anyplace else. Listen up.

Many years ago, my friend (I'll call her "Diana.") was just out of college and had zero money to spend on Christmas gifts for her loved ones. Did Diana wring her hands in anguish and despair? No. Did she go into debt in order to come up with something to put under the tree? Nuh-uh.

Diana went to the dump.

This sounds distasteful, I know, but Diana swears she found some terrific stuff at the dump. For instance, she came up with a very nice lamp. I didn't think to ask her about the shade, but apparently the lamp itself was pristine, or as pristine as something could be that came from a dump. She wrapped that lamp up and presented it to her parents, who, I can only assume, were none the wiser.

I can't say that I've ever shopped at the dump, but I *have* been creative during difficult financial times.

One year, for my husband's birthday, I got him a copy of John Updike's novel, *Rabbit is Rich*. Harry had been wanting to read that for some time. But, when he unwrapped it, and saw that I'd given him a twenty-dollar book, his smile was tempered by a wince.

We didn't have twenty dollars to spare. I know he was thinking about groceries, and the mortgage, and shoes for the kids. And then he flipped through the pages and came upon the salmon-colored card in the back. The card with the due-date stamped on it.

. . . it's possible that dump-shopping is more widespread than you thought.

I got this book at the library. Boy, was he relieved. His shoulders fell, and he sat back and grinned. Best gift I ever got him. He read the book and I returned it to the library two weeks later. No expense, no clutter—what's not to like?

However, if I had selected the Updike novel from a dump, I don't think I would have told Harry. Even in marriage— maybe especially in marriage—there are certain things that are better left unsaid.

After all, if someone gave *you* a gift that had been discovered in a dump, would you want to know that?

Come to think of it, there may be an item in your possession that was presented to you wrapped in fancy paper— something with a history you never suspected.

Look around. Those gloves you unwrapped last Christmas morning? The coffee mug? The lamp? You figured they were just shopworn, that your loved one held off on shopping until the last minute, and ended up with the display sample.

And maybe that's what happened, but I'm just saying that it's possible that dump-shopping is more widespread than you thought. Especially among kids in college, like my friend Diana. I like to think of it as a kind of hands-on lesson in economics.

However, should you find yourself Christmas shopping at the dump, take a look around and see if any of *my* kids are there. If they are, do me a favor: Give 'em a ride to the library.

MY SECRET ADDICTION

I have a confession to make. I have this . . . addiction. It involves needles, and drugs that make me mumble and drool. I don't indulge in this addiction every day. No, just a few times a year, when I have a hundred . . . well, maybe two hundred bucks that I can spare.

And then, when my daughter's at school, and my husband's at work, I sneak off to a neighborhood that otherwise I'd never go to.

I lie back and the needle dives in deep. Staring at the ceiling, I wait for the drug to overtake me. And then, *he* comes into the room. The man who has the power to perform magic, to turn back time.

It's my dentist. I used to show up maybe once a year, just to get my teeth cleaned. Then, one day I needed to have a filling replaced. One teeny little filling. He said—so innocent, "Would you like a metal filling, or a composite filling?"

"What," I asked, "is the difference?"

"Well," he said, sizing up the teeth that were no stranger to the dentist's drill when I was growing up. " . . . you *know* what silver ones look like. Composite fillings are, essentially, invisible. They just look like your tooth before you ever had a cavity."

Now, this was hard to believe. I said, "You mean those porcelain fillings that look chalky and fake and fall out?"

He just shook his head and said, "Think space-age."

And so, I took a chance and let him blast out my old gray filling and fill up the crater with his space-age stuff. He handed me a mirror and I was hooked. I couldn't believe what I was seeing; he had given me back the tooth I had when I was a kid.

More, I had to have more. I waited a few months until my first experience was paid for, then I was *drawn* back to that chair. I had to have another fix. Just two more this time.

Again, this magician—this wizard—handed me the mirror and again I was astonished at what I saw. I'm telling you, it's like a dream, or some cheesy movie where I'm this aging woman who makes a pact with Beelzebub who then restores my old, silver-plugged teeth to their virgin state.

I have been given a second chance. I'm not that same seven-year-old who used to grin at people with chewed-up Tootsie Roll stuck to my front teeth. And I can't remember the last time I fell asleep with my mouth full of Hershey Bar. I'll take good care of them this time, I swear.

I haven't had the courage to tell my husband about this addiction of mine. He still winces when I go and get my hair done. Imagine if he knew I was spending this kind of money on a cosmetic procedure . . .

One of these days, I'll tell him what's been going on. Although, he's probably wondering why I'm accumulating so many new toothbrushes, not to mention all those little dental-floss dispensers the size of a quarter.

I plan to tell him, I swear. Just not yet, because, what if he makes me stop? I can't stop now; I have three more teeth to go. Just three.

Plus, I'm starting to sort of enjoy the whole novocaine thing.

SILENT MEETING

My daughter goes to a Quaker school.

Now, a Quaker school is like any other school except for the fact that children are respected as much as any adult. And, once a week, they hold a silent meeting.

The first time I attended Silent Meeting, I was a little nervous, so I arrived a few minutes early. I settled into a metal folding chair, noticing how hard the metal was, and wondering how I would last for forty-five minutes with no one to entertain me. No one to talk to. No one to listen to. And you're *not* supposed to sit there and read or write, which are my two favorite diversions.

When I first sat down, I was tempted to fumble around in my pocketbook, maybe to find my checkbook and bring up the balance, or update my to-do list for the afternoon.

But I didn't do it. I didn't want to be caught by other early arrivals doing something wrong.

When it was time to assemble for the meeting, the kids and teachers arrived in twos and threes—and were silent from the moment they entered the building.

As people drifted in and found a spot on the floor or in

a chair, there was no shushing; there were no stern looks from teachers.

And then, all one hundred and eighty of us just sat there.

Hm. I wasn't sure I could last through forty-five minutes of this. A few minutes passed before I discovered something: That the silence at a Quaker meeting isn't just the absence of talking. It was this *thing* that rose up among us; I could feel it.

How does this happen? I think it's because *this* silence is intentional. It's not a lapse in conversation or a technical difficulty. It's not, as they say in radio, dead air. The purpose, I think, is to clear away distractions because, what is it that we're trying to distract ourselves from, anyway?

At the time of this meeting, my mind was staggering under a heavy burden. Someone I love was in big trouble and I didn't want to talk about it. My silent prayer at that meeting was to ask, without words, for everyone in the room to pray for—to choose—a happy outcome to this unbearable situation. As my thoughts radiated out into that room, my body felt lighter, my shoulders relaxed, the tightness in my throat disappeared.

I couldn't shake the feeling that this problem had, on some level, already been solved for me.

As the clock raced toward the end of our time together, I tried to get a handle on what was happening. (As always, I'm not happy until I can stuff my thoughts into words.)

Here's what I came up with:

That room was alive with energy, and it didn't matter whether any individual was a child or a grownup, it was all the same thing. Like stars, we were *radiating* energy.

And there was this overwhelming feeling that there were no divisions among us. That we all shared one big spirit.

Now, I have spent a good chunk of my life installed on a pew in church and never experienced anything like this. It felt as though I had, for the first time, turned off the lights and discovered the stars.

All too soon, everyone stood up, people smiled, and conversations began.

And, the problem that I'd brought into that room—in time, it disappeared.

LIGHTS OUT, EVERYBODY

My mother's a night owl. Every night, not only does she make it all the way through Jay Leno, but by the time Conan O'Brien comes on, her eyes are sparkling and she's ready to break out the Coke and snacks. Mum comes alive late in the day—she blossoms in the dark.

And, surprise, surprise, she doesn't exactly get up with the chickens every morning. Ten o'clock is more like it.

You're thinking: Who cares? I'll tell you who—her neighbors. These ladies are tucked in for the night by nine o'clock. So, of course, they're up before dawn, and they cluck among themselves about my mother, because her curtains are still drawn, and her porch light stays on past ten in the morning. Scandalous!

Let's face it. Early risers are unbearably self-righteous— I bet they invented self-righteousness. I suppose morning people had a right to be sanctimonious before the invention of electric lights, back when daylight farm labor was essential to survival. No sense burning candle wax when there are seeds to be planted and cows to be milked when the sun comes up.

The thing is, now that farming isn't exactly the most popular way to earn a living, some of us can't seem to quit feeling smug about sticking to this ingrained schedule.

And it makes us uneasy to think that while we're off-guard and sleeping, someone could be tiptoeing around, doing God-knows-what.

This is why people are clamoring for curfew laws. In Charlottesville, Virginia, we have a curfew, and the police enforce it. And lots of people think it's a good idea. Of course, they're probably all early-risers, so naturally they think it's reasonable to pass a law requiring that everyone under seventeen be confined within their houses between midnight and five A.M. After all, why should these kids be out after midnight?

Well, maybe they've been ice skating at the rink that closes at midnight and want to stop somewhere for a Coke and a snack.

Maybe they want to walk to the clearing at the end of their street and have a look at the stars.

That's just too bad. Good kids, with good parents, are home long before midnight, tucked in their beds. Right? I don't know about that—most crimes committed by juveniles happen between three and six in the afternoon. Does that mean we should keep them locked up twenty-four hours a day?

Thanks to this law, anyone who looks younger than seventeen had better be prepared to show identity papers to any police officer whose path they cross after curfew.

Are you a baby-faced twenty-five-year old? Don't get caught without your valid ID. You could be stopped for questioning and detained until you can prove your date of birth.

You don't even have to do anything wrong. To be young and visible after midnight is a crime in Charlottesville, unless you can prove that you meet the criteria for one of the exceptions, such as an emergency errand for a parent.

Even then, every single police officer that you encounter in the course of your errand has the right to stop you and haul you off to the police station for questioning.

Is this the kind of country we want to live in?

If we allow laws to be passed that require us to be off the street by a certain hour, then what's next? Bed-checks by the city police? If so, my mother's in for big trouble. If breaking out the Coke and snacks after midnight becomes a crime, then slap the handcuffs on her. This is one liberty that she's unlikely to give up without a fight.

WHAT HEARTBREAK FEELS LIKE

Your blood pressure falls. You're shaking so bad you can hardly hold onto the phone. You're too weak to stand, too weak to sit. You slide down onto the floor.

This is what heartbreak feels like. Surely, everyone has experienced heartbreak. But, for those of you who have *not* felt this way, for those of you who have done this to the rest of us, this is what it feels like:

Lying on the floor, the phone still in your hand, you make a pathetic attempt to mask your grief, to sound normal. But the huskiness in your voice betrays you.

You say, "I understand. Really. I'm okay. No, look, I think this is for the best. You're right. Yes, yes, of course, we'll always be friends."

Oh, right, friends. That's the worst part. What you want to say is: Look, my friends don't rip my heart out, stomp on it and set fire to it. My friends don't tell me they don't want to see me anymore.

I used to think that a happy marriage would erase those old wounds, make me mentally healthy and evolved.

Hah. All it takes is a movie, or a friend's crisis, or just an empty afternoon to set me to brooding all over again.

A few months ago, I was sitting on the couch, leaning up against my devoted husband and reading the newspaper over his shoulder, when I came across an article about Carroll Spinney, the fellow who plays Big Bird on *Sesame Street*.

In the article, he tells of the time when his wife left him, and he was so heartbroken that he found himself weeping inside his Big Bird suit. Sobbing, inside his Big Bird suit.

Doesn't that story bring every heartache you've ever had right back to the surface?

Many's the time I've struggled to hide behind a mask of bravery and go on with life, as though my heart were *not* hemorrhaging. It doesn't work. Instead, I become transparent. Sorrow infuses my every movement, my every word. I am marinating in grief, and I fool no one.

And in this twisted state of mind, I'm hoping that someone comes along and rips *his* heart out someday. Someday soon.

Is this love? I don't think so. I'm not sure what it is. But the memory of it makes me powerfully grateful for my happy marriage. Today, memories are all that remain of old heartaches. Now, I can give the *appearance* of a woman who is evolved and unshakable in her contentment.

But all it takes, even while cuddling up and sharing a newspaper, is a story like the one about Carroll Spinney crying inside his Big Bird suit, and it all comes back.

If the truth be known, it never really went away.

I don't know what the future holds, but I'd like to know where I could get my hands on a Big Bird costume, just in case.

PART FIVE

BIRDSEED AND A HOT DOG

BIRDSEED COOKIES

I took one bite of that cookie and knew there was something in there that I'd never tasted before. It was crunchy—I hoped it was something edible.

My son, Jack, was in ninth grade. He had taken over my job as cookie-maker. But did he aspire to make cookies just like mine? Uh-uh. He was a teenager. The job of a teenager is to look at the world and say, "I can do better than this!"

He saw the way I made cookies—always the same, always following the directions on that yellow bag—and he sought to improve on it.

For him, a recipe is to baking what a musical score is to a jazz musician: something that begs for improvisation.

If it was in the kitchen, it could end up in his cookie dough. Pine nuts, oregano, Worcestershire sauce, curry, whatever.

The more poker-faced Jack appeared, the more outlandish the ingredients. One of his more successful experiments involved cayenne pepper. It was not overpowering, but these were cookies that made you stop and think.

Jack takes the same joy in baking that I do. I've always

loved having an oven with a window, so I can watch the lumps of dough slowly melt, and spread, and puff. Once, while sitting on the kitchen floor next to Jack as we peered through the oven window, he said, "I like this part. Right here . . . where they're maxed out on puffiness, and they start to collapse. It looks like they're breathing."

That's mah boy.

In our family, the worst insult you can give someone's cooking is to say that it's "memorable."

Jack made quite a few batches of memorable cookies. One unforgettable attempt involved adding too much butter and oil. We watched through the tinted oven window as the pale circles flattened, spread, and fused into one stiff, brown rectangle.

What a waste of good ingredients. Why can't this kid just follow directions, like everybody else?

And then, Jack started swinging a hammer down on the cookie sheet.

He looked up at me, triumphant, and said, "Cookie-brittle."

But then there was that time with the crunchy mystery ingredient. I chewed slowly, cautiously. What was it? Jack had a twinkle in his eye that was nearly audible. He was loving this.

"C'mon, Jack. What is it?"

All I got from him was a hysterical giggle. When I put down the cookie, he quickly picked one up and ate it, proof that it was safe.

Through a mouthful of mystery cookie, he said, "Don't worry. It's not, like, sand or anything."

Sand? I hadn't thought of sand.

His parakeet was squawking in the other room. Jack glanced toward the sound and allowed a lopsided grin to give him away.

I shook my head slowly and said, "No . . . "

He nodded his head ever so slightly.

"You didn't."

By now, he was laughing so hard he had to support himself against the kitchen counter.

I wasn't sure he could hear me over the sound of his own laughter, but I shouted, "*Birdseed?* Jack, you put *birdseed* in the cookies?"

He was palming the tears from his eyes as he said, "It's food. . . . "

I don't believe I would ever eat birdseed cookies again. But, if the truth be told, they weren't bad.

BROTHER, COULD YOU SPARE A DIME?

I'm sitting at a table at Greenberry's, nursing a cup of coffee—a cup of coffee that cost me a dollar and thirty cents—as I wait for my son to have his hair cut next door.

When I paid for the coffee, I only had a dollar fourteen and had to borrow sixteen cents from my son.

I open up the house copy of the *Washington Post*, and on the second page there's this ad for Burberry trench coats.

These coats cost a small fortune, as everyone knows, but they *are* made well, and they're sturdy . . . plus all that other stuff that people say in order to justify an outrageous price.

I'd be delighted to own one.

In the ad, a lovely young woman is striding through some kind of pasture. I look closer at the ad and see that the lovely young woman in the seven hundred and ninety-five dollar coat is holding something. It blends in very well with her coat and it's hard to make it out.

There's a face—it's a dog! A dog wearing a trench coat. A teeny-tiny doggie trench coat.

. . . poodles can handle that sort of thing.

And the doggie trench coat costs two hundred and forty bucks.

You should see the look on this dog's face. It is mortified. It's not a poodle—poodles can handle that sort of thing, they're used to having mentally-unbalanced owners who put ribbons on their ear hair (how would *they* like that?) and clip them to make their hips look all poofy and fluffy.

No, this is a regular old dog. I kind of hope that right after this picture was taken, the dog jumped down and rolled around in cow poop. Do you suppose a Burberry raincoat is impervious to cow poop?

My son still isn't back from getting his hair cut, and my coffee's all gone. I hope the barber isn't putting little bows in his hair and making him all poofy.

I'm feeling like a bum, hogging a table when I've finished my coffee. I check my wallet again, hoping that I've overlooked some folding money that may have slid down out of sight. But there's nothing.

I pick up the paper again and decide that I would like to

meet the person who would pony up two hundred and forty bucks for a trench coat for his dog.

In fact, I'd like to meet him right now. Maybe he'd buy me a cup of coffee.

CELEBRATION

It was a hot, muggy day in midsummer. Fat, white clouds were billowing upward, but the forecast didn't call for storms.

In our cool, air-conditioned townhouse, it was time to celebrate. This was a happy day—our twins' second birthday. Our sense of celebration was magnified by the survival of one of our twins, Jackson, from his first birthday to his second. We were celebrating, my husband and I, and we were profoundly thankful.

Three weeks before that first birthday, Jack had been hospitalized for removal of a kidney that had grown to the size of a grapefruit. (Harry and I knew about watching for diaper rash and colic, but tumors? It just looked like Jack had a cute, round belly. I don't think Dr. Spock had anything to say about tumors.)

The pathologists disagreed: Was it benign or malignant? To be on the safe side, Jack endured seven months of chemotherapy. Even his eyelashes fell out.

So there we were, all set to celebrate their second birthday. Neighborhood kids have joined us around the table and everyone, including me, is wearing a party hat.

It's cake time. I step into the kitchen to light the candles. But before I succeed in getting the match to light, the phone rings.

It's Dr. Pearlman, our avuncular and unflappable pediatrician. There's a tightness in his voice, a sense of urgency I've never heard before.

He's talking about Jackson's chest x-ray, the one he had at his check-up the other day.

There's static on the line, crackling from distant storms.

Dr. Pearlman tells me that there's a shadow on the x-ray—a shadow on Jack's lung and how soon can I get him back to radiology so they can take more x-rays?

I'm staring down at the little holes in the mouthpiece of the receiver, wishing I could make myself very small, become a pinpoint, and hide in one of those little holes.

I know what this means: It *was* cancer and it has spread to his lungs and Jack won't live long enough to blow out three candles.

Before he hangs up, the doctor says that there's a possibility that the shadow was a problem with the x-ray itself, and not with Jack, but I can tell from his voice that he doesn't think so.

I will not go out there—to the dining room with the balloons and the party table with the paper table cloth and matching plates with Mickey Mouse grinning up at us—and tell my husband what I was just told. Not now.

I take a deep, ragged breath and turn my attention to striking the match. My hand is shaking as I light the candles. One . . . and two. That's it.

The kids have gotten impatient and rowdy, waiting for the party to begin.

They fall silent as I appear at the doorway, holding the illuminated cake. I am amazed to discover that, in spite of the painful lump in my throat, I can't help but smile.

Two parents, two babies . . . two flames.

STICK 'EM UP

It's Monday morning. My cup of coffee has not kicked in yet, and I'm *trying* to think straight, but it's not working. There's just too much going on in my life. And this morning, I don't know which way is up.

Stickies, that's what I need. I go to the kitchen, hoping to grab my pad of Post-It Notes.

I don't know how I ever organized my life or got anything done before they invented stickies.

I always buy them in bright colors—like flame orange or electric yellow—figuring they'll be more effective at reminding me of . . . whatever.

-check-up: 2 PM
-get pantyhose
-pick up Jill at school.

I even have one that's been on my dashboard for days now. It says, "Cheer up, things will get better." I actually feel better every time I glance at it.

But now, I reach for the pad of orange stickies—I know it was here last night, I remember wiping flour off it—but it's not there. In the junk drawer? I root around. No stickies. In

the other junk drawer? You couldn't fit anything else in that
drawer if you tried.

It's time to go. How will I remember to get that gallon of
milk? And tofu, I'll never remember tofu. Quick, find a scrap
of paper, find some tape. Forget the tape—that disappeared
ages ago. Why is there never anything handy when I need it?

My daughter's in a panic: She's late and it's all my fault.
It's always my fault.

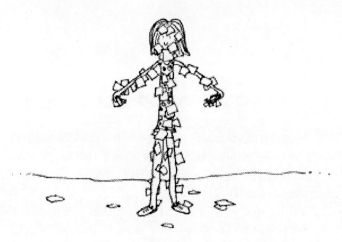

It would sure get the doctor's attention, don't you think?

I sling my purse over my shoulder and run for the car,
chanting, "milk and tofu, milk and tofu, milk and tofu . . . "

For someone like me who has a lousy memory, stickies
are a substitute for a frontal lobe—they are my mental prosthesis.

I stick them all over: on the steering wheel, on my pocketbook, on the front door. At home, I'll even slap a sticky on
my chest, so I'll remember to stick it on the dashboard when
I go shopping.

One time, I had written, "toilet paper" on a sticky, stuck
it on my chest, and forgot that I was wearing it. About an hour
later, my husband walked up to me wearing a sticky on *his*

chest that said, "bathroom." He said, "Oh, I thought we were playing a word-association game."

Yeah, right.

I have even considered festooning myself with stickies when I go for a medical checkup. I've never actually done this, I swear, but don't you think it would be a good idea to place a sticky, for instance, on my back that says, "What do you think about this mole? Looks suspicious to me." and draw a little arrow pointing to it.

Or one on my knee that says, "This aches sometimes for no apparent reason."

This would be much more effective than a list. It would sure get the doctor's attention, don't you think?

There are so many things we need to be reminded of— more than just to pick up something for supper. We should have stickies around that say, "relax," or "rejoice." Or, "listen." Maybe a sticky on the bathroom mirror that says, "appreciate."

Come to think of it, chances are I'll remember to buy that bottle of milk without a written reminder, but the one on my dashboard, the one that says, "Cheer up, things will get better."—that's the kind of reminder I need to see in writing.

PUP ROAST

To hear my daughter howling, you'd think I was roasting a live puppy on a spit. Jill was seven years old, and having a difficult evening, but this was the last straw. She peered through the window and saw her puppy dog, Sassy, paws-up on the center rack of the turned-on oven.

It was late on a school night. A few hours earlier, I was wiping the last saucepan dry after a long day that followed an endless week of family illness. All three kids, plus Mummy, had come down with some nasty virus. We took turns burning up with a 103-degree fever, passing it like a torch along the upstairs hallway, bedroom to bedroom.

Tonight, all foreheads were cool and I was ready for a relaxing evening. I imagined myself sprawling on the couch, staring toward the TV in a grateful stupor.

I was putting away the saucepan when Jill wandered in, scratching her head. You didn't need a magnifying glass to see the lice frolicking in her waist-length, honey blonde hair. These were not nits: These were the real thing. Full-blown cooties.

Forget the couch . . . and the TV.

It was just past nine o'clock—time for a trip to the pharmacy for toxic shampoo and a fine-toothed comb.

In case you're among the anointed few who have never had to deal with head lice, here's what happens:

First, you inspect every head in the house and supervise the application of the bug-killing shampoo.

Then, you strip every bed, and the washing machine and dryer churn steadily through the night as you wash every single sheet, blanket, comforter, pillow, towel, and article of clothing in hot water.

You wish you were rich so you could toss out everything in the house and start over.

Now, water hot enough to kill lice is hot enough to ruin most anything you wash in it.

There are some things that are just too fragile and precious to throw in the washing machine. Like stuffed animals. According to conventional lice-management wisdom, you should quarantine stuffed animals by sealing them up in a trash bag for at least two weeks. By then, any nits or lice will have died.

As I twisted the top of the bag and sealed it with duct tape, Jill had tears in her eyes, worried that her stuffed pets wouldn't be able to breathe in the plastic bag.

Now, I know my kids well enough to predict that taking away *all* the stuffed animals of my seven-year-old—for any reason—would one day land her on the BarcaLounger of some sympathetic therapist, reaching for the Kleenex and telling tales of Mommy dearest.

So, while Jill was upstairs finishing her shower, I liberated from the trash bag her most beloved stuffed animal of all, Sassy the puppy, and put her into the oven on low heat. That would kill any nits in a matter of minutes, and Jill would have her favorite puppy to comfort her through the night.

And I would have gotten away with it if she hadn't come downstairs so soon.

And, if our oven didn't have that stupid window.

She stood in the doorway, pink and glowing from her shower, a tiny figure in a Hello Kitty nightshirt.

Jill's eyes went straight for the oven window where she came upon the nightmare vision of faithful, sweet Sassy roasting in the oven. Oh, the look on her face . . . It was a study in horror and betrayal.

Ah, well, it looks like the BarcaLounger, the therapist, and the Kleenex are in Jill's future, after all.

THE CHINA SYNDROME

When you're young and broke and they tell you it's time to pick out a china pattern because that's what you do when you're planning a wedding, it can be a strange, paradoxical experience.

English bone china or American china?

Gold rim or plain?

Floral or geometric?

My son, Jackson, is engaged to be married. The wedding is a ways off—not till next summer—so there's a good year in which to obsess about such things.

Although, if the truth be told, my son, and Tricia, his fiancée, are far more concerned with finishing college than with daydreaming about wedding gifts.

Give them time.

Twenty-two years ago, *I* was the fiancée.

It was unreal, that whole scene. Independent me, maverick me, getting married. Furtively flipping through *Brides* magazine, a magazine I had scorned only weeks before. Scouring bridal shops and department stores for the perfect everything.

The college girl who'd never had a savings account in her life—and who'd spent the previous four years disdaining the bourgeoisie—was tip-toeing through the china and crystal department at Filene's, weighing the relative merits of the china pattern "Autumn" versus "Castle Garden."

Feeling way out of place in my peasant blouse and bell-bottoms, I made my way down the aisle, dangerously close to the sparkling breakables. My mother was teaching me how to hold a china plate up to the light and look for the shadow of my fingers right through the plate—a clever trick that tells you whether or not this china is the real thing.

Now, I'm the mother, and soon I'll pass along my own brand of clever tricks to Jackson and Tricia. I should probably tell them: You might want to avoid gold rims since you can't put them in the microwave. And, come to think of it, the teacups are awfully small and doesn't everyone use mugs nowadays?

And then I worry: Where will they keep it? Jackson broke every toy he ever got. I can't imagine him carefully hand-washing the china and storing it with protective circles of felt between each plate.

And this gets me to thinking: Why do we have this tradition of giving fragile gifts to young people who have no experience in caring for such things?

Why don't we give them plastic cups and paper plates? Things you can throw away or lose, and it won't matter all that much. Stick it in the microwave, toss it in the dishwasher. Drop it, throw it. Who cares?

But wait, maybe that's the point. Maybe that's exactly why we entrust newlyweds with china plates and crystal goblets. This is a tangible way to help them learn to take care of things that are precious and fragile.

For twenty-two years my husband and I have lived with our "Castle-Garden" china. We use it a lot, and so far, we haven't broken a single plate. There have been some close calls, but it's all there, intact and housed together in its own cabinet.

As Jackson and Tricia go through life together, I hope they handle their marriage with care, always mindful of how very precious and fragile a thing it is.

WALLOWING

I woke up. Where was I? Perky voices babbled from the TV; a bright bulb made me squint. I turned over to see if I was alone, and bottles rolled together and clanked. I rose up on one elbow to find I was the only one there.

The bed was strewn with empties and trash and magazines. My head throbbed while my stomach did a slow, sickening rollover.

Oh, right. My husband's out of town. My daughter's at a sleepover somewhere. All this had seemed like such a good idea last night—I just wanted to get in touch with my inner slob. The one I used to be when I was single.

You see, before I got married, supper was a time for a can of tuna and a fork. Maybe toast, if I was feeling ambitious. I loved going out to a restaurant for a big dinner, but if I was home, a bowl of cereal would do just fine.

And then, I married a man who is much more civilized than that.

What followed has been twenty-four years of thinking up something to put on the dinner table every blessed night– real meals, with vegetables and everything.

I know, this is a much healthier way to live, but it requires so much effort . . . and creativity that I'd rather channel into something else. Once in a while, anyway.

We live in the kind of house where you will never find a can of soda, or a bag of chips. Those things are a waste of money, and bad for you, to boot.

Anyway, that's been the party line for twenty-four years. This is what happens when you marry a sensible, civilized man.

So, when Harry reminded me that he'd be out of town last night, and Jill would be at a pajama party, I thought: Hot dog! For once, I can have dinner *my* way.

I went to the grocery store and got myself a six-pack of Coke–the real deal, no diet soda for me, not this time. And it had to be the kind that comes in those curvy, glass bottles.

I tossed a couple of bags of Cheez Doodles into my cart, thinking: Oh, I am such a bad girl . . . And, naughtiest of all, while waiting in the checkout line, I grabbed three or four women's magazines. You know, those magazines your mother used to read for recipes and fashion advice, but now, they've been taken over by Masters and Johnson instructors.

Back home, blissfully alone at last, I retreated to my bedroom, where I watched three videos in a row–videos that *I* picked out—while guzzling Coke and happily cramming Cheez Doodles into my mouth. When the movies failed to hold my attention, I read an article called "Twenty-One Ways to Drive Him Wild." And I'm thinking: Wait'll he finds this stuff in the trash, *that*'ll drive him wild.

And I had a great time . . . Until I woke up around two in the morning, like a hamster in my nest of magazines and plastic bags.

The TV was on, the lights were on, my head was throbbing, and my face and T-shirt were covered in orange Cheez-Doodle dust.

Oh, I have learned my lesson. Next time, I'll remember to turn off the light, *and* the TV before I fall asleep.

It's so much more civilized that way.

THE WALTONS GO TO
SOUTH PARK

Our friend, Kay, spent last weekend at our house. I said, "Let's go to Monticello." She said, " Let's go to the Waltons Museum."

Turns out, the only thing Kay ever watches on TV—and she watches it every night—is *The Waltons*. I should mention that Kay is a former nun who finds the real world to be heartbreaking.

And so, we went to the Waltons Museum in Schuyler, Virginia. As we pulled into the parking lot, Kay looked confused. We explained to her that the museum consists of a few sets recreated from the original *Waltons* sets in Los Angeles. It's not in that familiar farmhouse on TV; it's in an elementary school.

As we crossed the parking lot, she said, "This is not like it's supposed to be." And she looked so sad.

I pointed to the white house across the road and said, "I think that's the house that Earl Hamner, Jr. grew up in."

"Who?"

"Earl Hamner, Jr. He's the guy who wrote the TV show." And I'm thinking: How does she not know this?

Harry said to her, gently, "Kay, the show is fiction, you know."

I could hear her mind shifting gears. "Okay, but it's based on that man's life, isn't it?"

The conversation continued in this vein as we wandered through the museum, pausing reverently by the roped-off entrances to the Walton's kitchen, their parlor, and John-Boy's room.

On the ride back to our house, Kay told us how lucky we are because Harry and I have such a beautiful family, and that for her, we are the real Waltons, not what she's been watching on TV all these years. After all, through the growing-up years we were together every night for supper, and we took the kids to Mass and they all made their First Holy Communion.

Well . . .

That evening I got sick suddenly, and went to bed. (I like to think it was stomach flu and not guilt at allowing Kay to keep her misperceptions about our family. Everything she said was true, about supper and church, and all. But jeez Louise, no way are we the Waltons.)

Harry and Kay were in the study, below my bedroom. Swing music and jazz from the thirties and forties drifted up through the floor.

And then Jackson's car was crunching up our gravel driveway. He was home for the weekend. And I remembered what was supposed to happen next, but all I could do was lie there and groan.

All day, Waldo and Jill couldn't wait for Jack to arrive, because he was bringing a stack of videos . . . *South Park* videos. Had I not been so sick, I would have sprinted downstairs and begged Jack to have his *South Park* festival some other night. Any other night.

In case you've never heard of *South Park*, it's a cartoon that is emphatically for adults only. It's crude and violent . . . and very funny. I love to sit around with my grown children and watch *South Park* videos. However, I didn't especially want Kay to know this about our happy little family. Talk about disillusioned . . . To find out in the course of a single day that the Waltons are fake and that Harry and Janis's children have been raised by wolves. It's too much to bear.

Nearly paralyzed in my bed with nausea, I listened all evening to the twin soundtracks seeping up from downstairs: Harry and Kay's voices along with swing music from the study, and filthy *South Park* dialogue from the living room.

Please God, keep her out of the living room.

The next morning, I discovered that miraculously, Harry had managed to keep Kay away from the *South Park* festival in the next room.

So, there you have it. A story with prayer and miracles and family togetherness. Kay returned home with stories, no doubt, to tell about her weekend with a family just like the Waltons.

ZERO HOUR

A couple of weeks ago, the phone rang mid-morning. It was my husband at work. No big news, just a reminder about who'd be home for dinner, and should he pick up a loaf of bread, and by the way, the minivan's odometer turned over to 200,000 miles this morning.

I didn't want to let on that I was disappointed, but I was thinking: Oh, man. I've been driving that thing around for eleven years. Eleven years and I missed it.

Two hundred thousand miles.

I hung up the phone and thought about where my Plymouth Voyager has taken me. For one, it has taken me from my hectic, suburban existence in Maryland to my peaceful, happy life in rural Virginia. From driving past unbroken expanses of aluminum siding to driving through the most graceful, beautiful countryside I've ever seen.

My van has taken me from driving around my daughter's Brownie troop to driving around alone.

Taken me from the age of thirty-five, the mother of young children, to forty-six, the mother of children who have put me behind glass, for emergency use only.

I'm ambivalent about my van. I'd love to have something shiny and new. Something with airbags and a CD player.

On the other hand, wishing my van away makes me feel disloyal, as though I were trying to do away with a beloved, aging nanny—one who shepherded my children safely from home, to school, to birthday parties, and back home again—who witnessed arguments and fights and confessions while continuing to serve, silently, with mute confidence that all of us would grow up and be none the worse for any of it.

I tried to imagine what I'd just missed. Going from 199,999 every digit is displaced. I pictured the little numbers struggling to make way for the two and all those zeroes.

It was time to get a grip. Okay, I missed the big moment, but, so what? There's nothing intrinsically significant about the two hundred thousand-mile point.

Nevertheless, like the new millennium that's at our doorstep, it feels important because all those zeroes are *really cool*. When 2000 comes, I'm sort of looking forward to looping all those zeroes on checks and correspondence. They're round and smooth and there's something about all those zeroes that feels like a blank slate—a fresh start.

It even feels like a fresh start for my '87 Voyager.

The weekend after that phone call, I washed and vacuumed my van for the first time in . . . Well, I can't remember the last time I washed it.

I even considered treating it to a paint job. Theoretically, it's a *black* Voyager, but a good third of the paint has flaked away down to bare metal. Now, it's more like a silver Voyager.

Turns out, a paint job would cost around five hundred bucks, so forget that.

As I sat in the driver's seat, spraying Windex on the steering wheel and discovering the beige vinyl below the gray grime, I kept glancing wistfully at the odometer. It was dozens of miles past all those zeroes.

And I wondered: Will I still be driving this van when it turns over to *three* hundred thousand miles?

Good God, I hope not.

I'm about due for a fresh start, myself.

KEYS TO THE KINGDOM

By the time my twin boys were two-and-a-half years old, I was getting pretty good at bad-mummy shortcuts. Like, you don't have to give them a bath *every* day. Stuff like that.

I hated getting up at the crack of dawn just because the kids were up. So, in an attempt to catch a few more minutes of sleep, one night I put out two bowls of cereal on the kitchen table and covered them with tinfoil.

Now, I had taught the boys to read about six months before this, when they were two.

(Yes, when they were two. It is so easy to teach a two-year-old to read, you wouldn't believe it. I got a book called *How to Teach Your Baby to Read*, by Glenn Doman, and I just did it.)

So, one night when I was in lazy-mummy mode, I left out the cereal bowls and put a plastic bottle of milk in the fridge in easy reach of the little guys.

I taped a note to the TV that said, "Your breakfast is on the table. Just get the milk from the refrigerator and be careful when you pour it. I love you!" I think the "I love you" was my way of saying, "I can't believe how desperate I am for some extra sleep. I am so sorry . . . "

Anyway, I heard them when they went downstairs and I was pretty happy about not having to drag myself out of bed right away. They were giggling when they found my note. I had drifted back to sleep for a few minutes when Waldo came upstairs to give me a full report.

He said that they didn't make a mess, and then he said, "And I give Jackson and me our vitamins."

Now I was awake, let me tell you. They loved their vitamins—colorful and sweet and shaped like the Flintstones.

I flew down the stairs and found the open bottle on the counter. It was nearly full, thank God. When my heart stopped slamming around in my chest, I knelt down next to Waldo and said, "Honey, how did you get that cap off the bottle?"

He picked up the cap, and with the tiny finger of a two-and-a-half year old, he pointed to the raised letters on top, saying, "It says, 'push down and turn.'"

Ah, jeez. This is what happens when you teach them to read: You give them the keys to the kingdom. But that doesn't mean they have an ounce of good sense.

Years later, the boys got their learner's permits the very day they were eligible. I let them take the wheel a few times and, while *I* was nervous, they actually did pretty well. Nevertheless, I found myself offering to drive them wherever and whenever they wanted to go. I'd pick them up after work at midnight, get up before dawn to take them to school, whatever.

I knew they could learn how to drive, but it was that judgement thing again. Letting a sixteen-year-old drive a car unsupervised is like putting a two-year-old in charge of dispensing vitamins.

Waldo didn't get his license until he was eighteen and a half; Jackson was twenty. And, you know, that was just about right. That's when they were beginning to see the world through the perceptions of an adult.

That's when it was time to give them the keys to the *car.*

OH, MAMA,

TAKE A WHIFF ON ME

Here we go again; they're handing out cake. I really shouldn't have any.

This is the fourth birthday party at my house in two weeks. And there's always leftover cake. As the mother, I consider it my responsibility to help clean out the refrigerator. And so, I have a slice of cake, like, every hour or two.

I was convinced that my jeans were shrinking, but they haven't been through the laundry in some time. So, unless there's something about being tossed into a heap on the closet floor that causes denim shrinkage, it's time to cut back on the cake.

In order to bolster my flagging self-control, I have turned to an alternative weight-loss method—I sent away for these aromatherapy things. I'm using one right now. It's a plastic disk the size of an Oreo—you pin it to your shirt.

The plastic is impregnated with something that smells like . . . well, I'm not exactly sure what it smells like. But whenever I take a whiff, it brings me back to the mid-1950s when I picked up my father's hairbrush. It was one of those oldfangled guy-brushes with no handle. It smelled like plastic and hair oil. (My God, I'm old enough to remember men using hair oil . . .)

Anyway, it's not the kind of smell that gets you to thinking about food. And that's the idea: It's an appetite suppressant.

I've been using these things off and on for a few months now. My daughter, Jill, finds it embarrassing that I wear this red plastic brooch on my shoulder. So, whenever I'm going to be seen with her, I pin it to the *inside* of my shirt, and every now and again I stick my nose down into my collar and take a whiff.

When serious temptation beckons, I *keep* my nose tucked inside my shirt for several seconds. You'd think that would be more embarrassing to my daughter than just *wearing* the red button, but she doesn't seem to mind.

Jill has just appeared with a slice of cake on a plate—for me. After a longing look, I take a hit off the aromatherapy button, turn away, and say, "No thank you."

Oh, am I strong, or what?

. . . But jeez, I *made* that cake . . .

It's a recipe handed down from my grandmother—Nana Jaquith's chocolate cake—and I've never made it before. I should at least try a piece. Just to see how it turned out.

Erma Bombeck once said that she pitied all the women on the Titanic who were worried about their waistlines and passed up dessert that night. And it's so true—you never know how close you might be to an iceberg that has your name on it.

Plus, what difference will one piece of cake make? One teensy sliver of Nana Jaquith's chocolate cake.

I turn around and find that Jill is still standing there, holding out the plate. She figured it would be a matter of seconds before I changed my mind.

If the truth be known, the aromatherapy thing does work. It really does suppress my appetite. The thing is, I'm not gonna eat this piece of cake because I'm hungry. I'm gonna eat it because it tastes good.

THE BRIDE WILL NOW
TOSS THE STUNT BOUQUET

A couple of days ago, I was sick in bed. And while I was staring up at the ceiling, I figured that since I suddenly had all this free time, I might as well start helping my son to plan his wedding.

Last week Jackson and Tricia announced that they had set a date. And, you know the tradition about how the *bride's* family pays for everything? Well, I got a call from Tricia's mother the other day in which Colleen said, essentially: Forgettaboutit.

And so I reach down next to the bed and rummage through my growing heap of books, magazines, and newspapers. Where did I put that wedding book?

Aha. I open it up to a random page and find that I've landed in the flower chapter. I read a few pages and discover that there are endless possibilities when it comes to blowing a fortune on wedding flowers. Flowers for carrying, flowers for the altar, flowers for the pews, flowers to throw on the *floor*, for heaven's sake.

Rose petals strewn down the aisle sound nice until you realize that someone's paying a lot of money for people to stomp all over their flowers.

My wedding was nothing like that. As I recall, my only instructions to the florist were to make it cheap and simple. And he did. For today's bride, according to this book, *one* bouquet is not enough. You gotta have *two*. You get your real bouquet and then there's the stunt bouquet for throwing to the single girls. This is a smaller, cheaper version of the bridal bouquet.

Toss 'em the fake one, and you get to keep your real one.

Why does the bride want to hang onto her bouquet? What is she planning to do with it? I can see saving a flower or two to press into the Bible, but the whole thing? It'll just end up on top of a bureau somewhere, turning brown and gathering dust.

I'm wondering whether Heloise has any hints on recycling bridal flowers.

This throwing of an imitation bouquet strikes me as a crummy thing to do.

I'm not sure why I care so much. My fever is shooting back up. And my throat feels like it's been put through a shredder. Just holding the book is too much effort; I toss it over my shoulder, back into the pile.

Decades ago, I tossed my bouquet over my shoulder to a throng of eager young women. It was an arm bouquet of white carnations and ivy. I chose carnations because they're cheap and they smell good. Plus, when I was a kid and my father got flowers for my mother, it was always carnations. Probably because they were cheap and they smelled good.

There's a picture in our wedding album of Harry's sister, Sue, leaping way above everyone else to snag my bouquet. Today, when I think about what Sue did with those flowers, I thank God that it never occurred to me to toss some diminished, fake version of my bouquet.

When we got back from our honeymoon, I found out that the day after our wedding, Sue took my bouquet to the cemetery, and she searched for my father's grave so she could put my flowers on it.

Amazing, huh? As I drift off into a hot sleep, I wonder if Tricia plans to throw a fake bouquet.

Oh, man. I'm turning into a mother-in-law already. Somebody tell me to keep my mouth shut.

Sue took my bouquet to the cemetery . . .

THE BEST AND THE

BRIGHTEST, BANISHED

I nose my car into the single visitors' space in the school parking lot. I shift the car into park, and hesitate before turning off the ignition. I don't want to be here. Just looking out at that huge, sprawling building makes me queasy. And why are there no windows?

It's time for yet another meeting with the vice-principal, because there has been yet another problem with the school's computers, and he has rounded up the usual suspects. The usual suspects are my son, Waldo, and his friends.

These are playful, funny wiseguys. Intelligent kids who drive their teachers crazy because they're always asking questions the teachers have no answers for. And these kids are computer experts. The kind of people who—if we're lucky—will be running the world in a few years.

In short, these are the kind of kids that the vice-principal finds infuriating.

As my footsteps echo down the long corridor, I tell myself

to take a deep breath, to calm down.

The thing is, what I really want to say to the vice-principal is this: Leave my son alone. You blame him whenever anything goes wrong with a computer. You blame him and his friends because you are pathetically ignorant about computers. And you take out your ignorance and frustration on these kids. Stop it.

But I will never say any of this to him. He'd only take it out on my son.

Now, some parents I've talked to have no problems with this school. These are the parents of the athletes. Their kids are given the benefit of the doubt; bad behavior is shrugged off, even winked at.

I walk into the lab and find Waldo and two of his fellow computer geeks lined up against the wall. In front of them are the vice-principal and a computer consultant who has been called in to figure out what went wrong with the administration's computer. Important data has been lost, and the vice-principal is determined to find someone he can blame.

I stand apart from them and listen. The computer consultant is clearly exasperated with the vice-principal as he slowly reiterates that the administration's computer is not part of any network. It stands alone. It is impossible for a student to access it from any other computer.

Well, the consultant is dismissed, and the minute he walks out the door, the vice-principal announces that Waldo and his friends will be suspended from school for two days for hacking into the administration's computer.

I can't believe what I'm hearing.

And then the vice-principal says that Waldo's in even deeper trouble for planting a virus in the computer lab. Turns out, he'd used the Paintbrush program to *draw* a virus for Biology class. A biological virus.

This morning, while the vice-principal was snooping

around in Waldo's files, he found one named "virus" and said, "Aha! A computer virus!" I am not making this up. In this man's eyes, here was a computer, and here was the word "virus." What else was there to know?

Yes, of course, I'll protest this suspension to the principal, but it won't make one bit of difference.

SHOULD I

TAKE A BOW?

This morning, my son moved out of our house. He's nineteen years old and has rented an apartment.

I should be happy; my work is done. During all those exasperating scenes of child-raising: the whining, the tantrums, the screaming—and that was just *me*—through it all, I truly thought it would never end. From the moment our twins were born, we were all caught up in a whirlwind drama. At 7:45 this morning, it was over.

Both of our twins have now left home, and it feels like the end of a performance. The play is over, and we're waiting for the reviews to come in.

As Waldo carried his boxes out to the car this morning, I wanted to shout after him: I'm sorry I ever spanked you. I shouldn't have done that. And I'm sorry I made you eat your green beans.

I swore I'd never do any of those stupid things that other parents do.

I thought it would be so simple. Just read the child-care book and do what it says. But I'd find myself slamming down the book and yelling at the kids for interrupting me. My real kids were messing up my plans to be the perfect mother.

During pregnancy, I had visions of myself as Maria Von Trapp, dancing and singing across the hillside, followed by my adoring children.

Hah.

Whenever I would sit on my daughter's bed and sing, "Hush little baby, don't say a word—" Jill would hold her little hands over her ears and shout, "Don't sing, Mummy, don't sing!"

What I needed was a good scriptwriter, a director. Someone to whisper in my ear and tell me what to say, what to do next.

A few years ago, I came up with a brilliant improvisation technique. When at a loss for words, I ask myself: What do I *not* want to hear about at the Thanksgiving table twenty years from now? Do I want to hear Jill say to Waldo, "Hey, remember the time Mum made you eat that scallop and you threw up?"

And so, when Waldo came to me last year and asked for sixty dollars for an application fee to Harvard, I wanted to say, "Harvard? Oh, right!" Instead, I pictured our Thanksgiving dinner table in 2017, imagined my son saying, " . . . and I could have gone to Harvard. But no, Mum and Dad wouldn't part with sixty bucks."

I bit my tongue and opened my checkbook. Now he only has Harvard to blame.

We have been in rehearsal for two decades, and now that I'm getting the hang of it, they are writing me out of the script.

It's over. And no one is even applauding.

WHOOSH...

When my kids were little, we would sometimes lie down on a quilt in the backyard at night. We'd talk about the universe, and be on the lookout for shooting stars to make wishes on. There was always lots of time between shooting stars, opportunities to point out constellations to them. "See that bunch of stars over there? That's Gemini, and remember Cassiopeia?" Time to tell the kids about how when we look at the Milky Way we're looking into our own galaxy, and that even though it's imperceptible to us, the stars are moving all the time.

Back then, I felt like an oracle—the center of their universe.

One night, when the twins were six years old, the three of us lay clustered on the quilt, our eyes wide, not wanting to miss anything in the vast black-and-silver sky that enveloped us. I was expounding about light years, telling them that the light we were seeing left those stars thousands—or millions—of years ago.

That's when Waldo's voice rose up and told me something wonderful, something that had never in my life occurred to me. He said, "So, those stars aren't really there."

I didn't know what he was talking about. "What do you mean?"

"Well, after the light left those stars, the stars moved away. Maybe they don't even exist anymore, 'cause, how could we tell?"

This kid was six years old. Of course, he was right. Why hadn't I ever thought of that? Maybe all those stars have sputtered out and we just don't know about it yet.

My memories of those sweet evenings with the kids came back to me–vividly—last November, when the Leonid meteor shower was predicted to be a knockout.

I lay in the front yard in the middle of the night, bundled up against the cold. This time, I was alone. The twins are grown and gone. Apparently, I was lying on the wrong side of the planet, because I saw very few meteors that night.

But then, there was one fabulous one with a long, fat trail streaming behind it. The kind of meteor that should be audible, if the world made any sense.

The stars that night were wonderful. All that old light—memories of stars—imposed on the blackness, like a photograph, or a thought.

I'm burrowing deeper into the sleeping bag when another fat meteor *whooshes* across the heavens. No wonder they call them shooting stars. It really does look like a star that just broke free from its constellation, blazing its own path across the sky.

MUMRISE

Even now, I wonder: How did someone like me end up in a hot-air balloon?

When I sit down on a park bench, I find myself unconsciously feeling around for the seat belt. When my kids were little, I would have been happy to make them wear helmets while playing on the monkeybars.

But there I was, hanging in the air, high above the treetops, with nothing but a cloth bag and hot air to save me from a splattering death.

My husband and I had driven from our home in suburban Maryland and dropped our kids off at camp in Virginia. We were—for the first time—on vacation without children. Feeling giddy and footloose, we headed for a hotel in Charlottesville.

When we checked in, the clerk mentioned that balloon rides were available, right there, on the hotel lawn. All we had to do was get up way early, and pay them a whole lot of money. I tried to picture myself doing this–hanging in the air. No seat belt, no helmet, no airbag.

No way.

Although, without kids, there was no need to be a model of restraint. No need to behave like anyone's mother. I could rediscover my authentic self, the brave one who takes chances.

Well, not big chances. I've never jumped out of an airplane or anything. I suppose the only risky thing I've done is to date Harry for a mere six months before I married him. Not exactly hair-raising behavior.

Okay, so I've *never* been one to take chances. But I was ready.

I hardly slept the night before. I lay there in the unfamiliar bed worrying that 1) the balloon would crash-land and I would die, and 2) that I would oversleep and miss the balloon ride.

The next morning, before the sun was up, we found ourselves climbing into what looked like an enormous wicker picnic hamper. A fat flame blasted up inside the balloon and the ground fell away. We rose up and met the sun.

There was this odd sense of stillness–and no wind. It felt like we were stationary and the scenery was being rolled along beneath us, like a special effect in a movie.

The Blue Ridge Mountains were no longer a two-dimensional prop against the horizon—they were this bulky mass, changing shape as we rose higher. Slowly, silently we glided above trees and fields and houses, blurring the line between real and dreaming.

What would my kids think? Mum, the safety chief, sailing through the air in a basket, without so much as a shin guard–and loving it.

Back at the hotel, over cups of strong coffee, Harry said, "What do you want to do today?"

The balloon ride had opened up a new boldness in me, and my response changed our lives. That afternoon, we didn't tour Thomas Jefferson's Monticello, and we didn't stroll across the Lawn at the University of Virginia.

Instead, we met up with a real estate agent who showed us a piece of land.

And we bought it.

We moved our family from suburban Maryland to the foothills of the Blue Ridge Mountains in Virginia—a happy, irrational decision made while gliding over the treetops in a basket.

That was ten years ago. This morning, I looked up and saw a hot-air balloon suspended in the air over my head. I like to think that there was someone in that basket having a thrill for the first time in a long while, and wondering what else she might be missing.

Printed in the United States
6882